WICKED SINS

SECRETS IN BLOOD
BOOK ONE

DANI RENÉ

Newsletter Sign Up

Want to keep up to date with all my new releases? Want a free book to devour? Sign up for my newsletter so you don't miss out on sales, new releases, recommendations, and much more!

FRANCO

There is a moment in every person's life that offers them the one thing they so hungrily search for to make them whole. Some fall in love, some land their dream job, and others find happiness in their solitary lives.

For me, it was the moment my father slipped a pearl-handled gun into my hand and allowed me to take a man's life. I watched in awe as the blood drained from his limp body. I smiled when his eyes flickered one last time with knowing. With the realization that he'd taken his last breath.

There was power in it.

I found my calling.

As I stepped toward my first victim, I smiled. He was the first person I'd snuffed out without blinking. I took the gold fountain pen that still sat in the top breast pocket of his navy-blue designer Tom Ford suit. When I brought it up to my face, I noted the droplets of his blood on the object and smiled.

You can't take from the dead, Franco, my father uttered from behind me.

His hand on my shoulder grounded me as I slipped the pen into my pocket, then turned to him. *Si, non ne ha più bisogno.* I told him that the dead man has no use for a pen in hell.

That's the moment I earned my nickname.

My father lovingly gave it to me as a fifteen-year-old boy and from that moment to this, as I lean in and meet the cold dead eyes of my victim once more as a thirty-eight-year-old man, I smile and tell him, "You've now met The Keeper. I trust you'll remember my name in hell." And pull the white handkerchief from his pocket and stuff it into mine.

I no longer have to look at the objects to know that I sprayed their blood on each item I take. Because I ensure the bullet hits just right, allowing my gift from the dead to be covered in the ruby-colored liquid of my new possession.

PROLOGUE
RAINA

"Dad," I call, racing into the study to find my father hunched over a box. He's rifling through papers and documents in such a rush I'm not sure he's even heard me enter. "Dad," I try again and he startles, spinning to face me.

"Rai, come in, baby girl." He offers me the warm smile I've grown up seeing on his face. My father is almost sixty, but he can pass for fifty. Even though he's getting older, he still keeps up with me.

I had my eighteenth birthday a few months ago, which has allowed me some freedoms, but he still monitors me. I'm the only child still at home. Growing up, it was just my brother and me. However, I'm thankful my older brother is no longer living at home. At thirty, he said he needed to venture out into the real world. What I think he meant was he didn't want Dad watching what dangerous things he was doing.

I'm close to my parents, but it's Andrea, my brother, who I've never been able to be around for longer than a family dinner. There's a darkness that surrounds him and it scares me. When he finally left home, it was as if I had lifted a weight from my shoulders.

"What are you doing home so early?" he questions with a frown.

"I finished up classes early. There wasn't anything going on after, so I figured I'd come and see if you needed any help. You know I enjoy doing your filing." It's a lie, but it easily slips from my lips. A terrible feeling had twisted in my gut when I was in English class, so I asked if I could leave. Since I'm ahead in class, Mrs. Drummond said it's okay.

From a young age, I knew my father was involved with dangerous men. Even though he's always kept it hidden, I stumbled across documents years ago that I knew gave away my father's connection to our ancestors.

I have always connected the Lombardi name with the Nostra, and even as a young girl, I understood what darkness lies in my family's history. My father, the man who does the accounts for a dangerous organization, can no longer hide his secrets from me.

Daddy has been good to keep me safe, but I have a feeling Andrea has already taken a walk down the sordid path. And as much as I know our father wants to protect us, I've already stumbled into that life without even knowing it.

They're all dangerous.

Violent men. The kind you see on the television who hurt people.

We're part of the *familia* and there's nothing we can do to stop it or to change our destiny. I know it, my parents know it, and soon I'll have to walk that fine line of right and wrong.

"Come in, Raina, sit." Daddy gestures to me to take a seat in the comfortable chair only inches from where he's busy. I curl onto the sofa instead and watch him. He offers another heartwarming smile and carries on what he's doing. Then continues to speak to the box of documents rather than me, "I'm finishing up some work here, then I have a meeting," he says easily but doesn't meet my eyes.

I know the meeting my father is talking about. He'll go to see *them*. The names of these men are not new to me and if you asked me to recite them, I'd be able to do it with no list.

"I was wondering if I can make us dinner tonight. The whole family together for once?" My question stills him for a moment before he shakes his head.

Turning my way, he responds with guilt shining in his eyes. "Not tonight, baby girl. I may not be home until late. Your mother is meeting her friends for bingo, so it's just you." His voice causes a shiver to race over me. There are many times that my father stays out late, but something about his tone makes me fearful.

"What are you doing, Dad?" I rise, stepping closer to him so I can look into those green eyes that match mine. "Tell me," I implore.

"You know my life isn't easy, Raina. Tonight, I have a meeting with an organization who can help me. They'll be able to assist with the accounts I've been in charge of with the companies who hired me. I want to take on less responsibility as I get older, and this meeting will allow me to plead my case."

"Are you meeting the Nostra?"

My father glances at me, shock clearly written all over his face. "What? I don't know what you're—"

"Dad, please?" I plead as he looks at me, and I can tell he's trying to find a way out of this conversation without admitting to what I already know. "Don't lie to me."

"Raina—"

I step closer to him, stopping when his brows rise in surprise. "Tell me the truth. I don't want more lies and secrets. This life... Our life... You need to tell me the truth. I'm an adult now."

He lowers his gaze to the floor. The guilt on his expression has my chest twisting and my stomach tight with anxiety. "You shouldn't know about this, Raina. You're far too young to even be talking about them. Even though this is our family legacy, I want them to keep you out of it. You're innocent."

"What about Andrea?"

He sighs sadly. Those eyes that offered me solace now hold apology. "He's in this life now, no matter what."

Nodding, I step back from him with a sense of doom knotting my stomach. It feels as if there's a serpent twirling itself around my organs, squeezing the life from me.

"I love you, Raina. You're a strong young woman and I only want what's best for you." His words hold my heart, weaving themselves around me. "Now go enjoy time with your friends and I'll see you later. Okay?"

"I love you too, Dad." Leaning in, I wrap my arms around him, giving him a hug so tight and so fierce, trying to remember what it feels like when he holds me because it's as if this will be the last time I'm ever in my father's arms.

My mind is racing a million miles a minute as I leave the office. Thinking of the names of the men Daddy works for, I wonder who exactly he's meeting with. They're all killers, volatile men who do horrific things.

I tiptoe through the house, settling myself on the sofa in the main living room. I glance out the window, watching the gardener work in the blistering sun. Summers in Los Angeles are my favorites. I love the sunshine, the heat. It reminds me of happier times before I knew about the evil that lives in this world.

The clouds are pulling over, an omen as far as superstitions go. Those gray clouds turn even darker and I want to run to my father, forbid him to go, but I know nothing will stop what's going to happen tonight.

The silence of the house keeps me tense. My stomach is in knots. Then I hear the footsteps of my father as he makes his way to the exit, and I know he's heading to the garage, which is only a few hundred meters away from the barn door of our family kitchen.

I know there's more tension in this house than there is in a heist. My mother knows there is more going on beneath the surface of what my father has offered. I overheard the fighting one night, months ago, about a promise. A vow. I don't know the details, but there was something scary in the way my mother uttered those two words.

Perhaps that's why my father is so adamant about hiding things from me. I found all my daddy's secrets. And while I've seen what they've done, I wasn't as fearful as I thought I'd be. That makes me as bad as them. I'm as evil as they are with things I keep hidden.

Before I can tell him anything more, my phone buzzes. When I check the screen, I see his name.

The man I've been seeing.

We're not dating. We're not a couple.

He's a secret. My darkest sin.

He's a wicked man, but it doesn't stop me from wanting him.

If anybody knew I was meeting him, I'd be in trouble. But he makes me tingle in places I want to tingle. He makes my body heat. And my panties? He makes them wet. I know there's something wrong with me. At least, I think it's wrong, but he makes me feel like it's right. He tells me girls like me need it. They crave it.

And I do.

When I wake up from my dreams of what we do, my hand is between my thighs. I'm a naughty girl and I do risqué things. I've learned from the men my father brings in here and seen them with women. They think the basement is off-limits, but they don't know that the code was easy to decipher.

When I'm alone, I go down there and watch the videos they record. The dirty things they do. Those filthy words they call the women. And I get myself off. Because I'm a bad, sinful girl.

My body likes the darkness.

I revel in it.

Only.

It's my secret.

And I keep it locked away.

I

FRANCO

The warehouse I enter is cold. My suit doesn't offer much warmth from the cold East Coast winters, and when I'm working on this side of the country, I keep myself aware by reveling in the iciness. It allows me to feel the rigidness of my blood. Soon enough, once the job is done, I'll fly home to L.A.

It's been years since I made my first kill. But with each person who falls victim to me, I know it's the only thing in my life that makes sense. To fulfill my father's dream, to step into his shoes and make sure that people know if they fuck with us, they won't survive.

No mercy.

No second chances.

When my cousin told me about this place, I thought he was making shit up, but as soon as I enter with Giovanni and Matteo flanking me, I can't deny that Lucio was right. Even though he's a Russo, I trust him more than his godforsaken brother, Cristiano.

There's a stench in the space, something you get accustomed to when you're in my line of work. It no longer bothers me, the darkness, the filth. It's life.

"Franco Moretti?" The asshole knows it's me when I step into the smaller room in the left corner of the warehouse. Lucio told me the man isn't going anywhere and when I reach the nark, I find him bound to a chair in the middle of the large open space. The office we're in is large, but the smell of urine and shit overpowers the space. "Please, we can pay." His voice grates slowly over my skin. The movement is as if he'd taken a blunt razor and attempted to shave me.

I hate it.

I loathe it.

But I stalk closer because he's staring at me like I'm his savior. I've never been one and I don't intend to be a fucking holy man now. I watch him in silence, pinning him with a glare. This asshole thinks he can lie, steal, and cheat the Nostra. That wasn't his first mistake, though. He used our shipment to deal in people, women. That's something I don't condone, and it's something I ensure never happens in my organization. I may not be a good man, but I don't sell people.

"I-I'll g-give y-you a-a-anything," he utters, and something about his fear makes me want to shatter every morsel of hope he has. Not because I'm evil, but because I'm standing here in front of my brothers, because I love the anguish on my mark's face. I need them to see what this life is really like. I don't sugarcoat shit.

"You know, Bruno"—I turn to him, leaning on my elbow on my knee as I press my shiny black shoe on his cock—"I hate when people lie." I'm posing like a fucking pirate on a barrel of rum.

"P-Please," he utters once more, but I bring the knife to his chin and slowly slice away a chunk of flesh, which falls onto his stomach. The blood that splatters over my Italian dress shoes only makes me smile. When I was younger, I would lose my shit, I'd curse, and lose my cool, but life has made me colder. I've learned to restrain my anger, to keep calm.

"You're getting worse," Giovanni mutters as he lifts the flesh and places it inside the container. Once the lid clicks closed, I glance at my brother and chuckle. "I'm serious, Franco."

"*Far parte del lavoro, fratello.*" I smile, telling my brother that it's part of the job. Pressing my foot down harder on the man's crotch, I listen to his wails of pain and agony, but it doesn't make me ease up because he doesn't deserve it. You fuck with the Nostra, you lose your life or your dick. It depends on how I'm feeling that day and what your crimes were. When blood pools on the floor where the chair is situated.

I watch my victim shudder as he bleeds out. I've ensured it's slow, painful, and as he splutters, I can't help reveling in the control I have over others. Things I want, I take. It's how I've always been. Those around me know I don't stop until the thing I've set my eye on is within my grasp.

My phone buzzes in my pocket, but I ignore it, knowing who it is. I've been expecting his call for days, weeks even. I know he'll call back or leave me a scathing message.

"Get this piece of trash out of here," I order my brother, Gio, while I wipe my blade with the clean white handkerchief. Tossing the material on the floor, I turn and walk out the door. Once outside, I pull my phone from my pocket and unlock the screen. There's a message from my cousin. Lucio Russo is the younger brother of my cousin, Luciano. Since the passing of their father only a year ago, I've been stepping in to help with their organization. Loading weapons onto containers and shipping them anywhere in the world.

The Russos are infamous for sourcing any arms you'd need or want. The Morettis are the complete opposite. You want something to take you higher than ever before, we'll get that for you.

Drugs and weapons are what we deal in. They go hand in hand beautifully and they offer us the income to live the life we have grown to enjoy.

I tap the call button and press the device to my ear.

"Franco." Lucio's deep timbre comes from the other end of the line. I expect him to sound as smug as he always does, but there's something off about his tone.

"Are you okay?"

"There's a shipment coming in at midnight. South Dock. I need you there," he informs me without responding to my question. That sets me on high alert.

"What the fuck is wrong? Why can't you do it?"

"There's also an envelope with all the information you need in my desk. Left-hand side, second drawer. You have the key."

"Lucio, I swear to God. *Dimmi cosa sta succedendo*," I order him to tell me what's going on using our mother tongue.

"*È necessario il tuo aiuto*," he tells me *your help is needed*.

Before I can respond, the line goes dead. When I try calling him again, the phone goes directly to a voice messaging service.

"Fuck!"

"What's going on?" Gio saunters out of the building toward me.

Shaking my head, I meet my brother's eyes. "I don't know, but we need to get to the Russo building right the fuck now."

He nods, and we slip into the car in silence. Gio drives, and Matteo watches me intently. I can tell he wants to ask, but I don't offer him an opportunity to because if I had to be honest, I'm concerned something is terribly wrong.

2

RAINA

The phone buzzes beside me while I attempt to study, but when I see his name, I can't not answer. Swiping my finger over the screen, I put the phone to my ear and listen a beat before answering. It's our secret code. "Hello." My greeting is tentative as I murmur into the microphone.

"*Bella*." The word is like a spark. It ignites every nerve in my body. "You're alone, yes?"

"Yes, Lucio." When I purr his name, the deep rumble of his growl is more than enough to have me dropping my pencil and allowing my eyes to flutter closed.

"I need you to listen to me, *Bella*." He calls me that because he said I'm beautiful. We've been doing this for far too long. This taunt and tease, back and forth. It's like a tennis match. He was my first. And with everything I offered him, he gave it back tenfold. When he took my virginity on my eighteenth birthday, I felt like I was floating. It hurt, I screamed, but I wanted him so much. Even though his mouth devoured me for an hour before he slid inside my body, I'd never felt pain like it.

Now that I'm nineteen and I've experienced him for

almost two years of my young life, I crave him like a drug. A hit of Lucio Russo is everything I need to survive. I know I shouldn't, but I have become obsessed with him. It's been four long years of me knowing him, and all I want is what he gifts me. The danger, the raw passion, and the lust.

Since I'm alone at home, I want to ask him to come to me, but I know he won't. There are rules in place for me and him. His world is dangerous, and he fits into it perfectly. But he's never put me in danger. Even though I hunger for adventure.

"Raina," he coos in my ear, caressing my name as if it's the most delicious thing he's ever tasted. "I want you to know you're special, *Bella.* Don't allow anyone to diminish your shine, your beauty. I needed to tell you this, so you know. I've had things happen and I'm going to need you to do something for me." He sounds serious, which sparks fear in my chest.

"You're scaring me, Lucio."

He doesn't respond immediately, but I say nothing more. I hear muffled voices on the other end of the line, and I'm certain he's busy. A moment passes, then he's back. "Listen to me. My cousin Franco will come to meet with your brother tomorrow. He'll explain everything."

"Oh? But why can't you just tell me now?"

More silence greets me, and I wait. The past few years have been like a cat-and-mouse game. He disappears, and I wait. Sitting silently in my room, I spend my time studying, but he's always in the back of my mind. Lucio Russo, the youngest capo since his own father had taken over the organization. I've heard of the cousins, the eldest, Franco, and the younger brothers, Giovanni and Matteo.

"Hold on, my darling," he tells me, then I hear a man speaking to him, but I can't make out what he's saying. Lucio responds, "*Sì, è stasera.*" *Yes, it's tonight.* When he speaks in his mother tongue, his accent is thick like syrup. But there's a huskiness to his voice that makes me shiver. The man is an animal. He's a murderer. He enjoys making people bleed. Once he told me he drained someone by hanging them from the ceiling of his warehouse and watched the blood drip from the slash in their neck.

I should be afraid of him, but I'm so far from scared. "Lucio." Once again, I whimper his name with fear lacing the word. Suddenly, my bedroom door flies open and I startle to find him standing on the threshold of my bedroom. "What—"

"I needed to see you just today. I was outside with my men when I called." He smirks like a devil. He walks like a predator. The perfectly tailored gray suit he's wearing fits his tall, lean frame. A black shirt below the suit jacket is immaculate with the silver tie.

His black hair is dark and styled in such a way that it looks like he's been tugging at it, and I wonder if he's been stressed, running his fingers through it. The dark five o'clock shadow that darkens his chiseled jaw shows he's not shaved this morning.

"How did you get in?" I whisper, my gaze locked on his.

The sinister smile on his face makes my stomach tumble. He's more than dangerous. He could so easily kill me. "You know I have access to you when I need it."

Shaking my head, I focus on the fact that he's here. It's a mixture of violence and lust. A shiver tracks through me, making me tremble, and I can tell from the look in Lucio's gaze how much he enjoys my unsure thoughts.

"I thought you were away?"

His gaze settles on my legs that are bare because I'm wearing a pair of jean shorts.

"I'm here for a meeting and I wanted to see my girl." While he speaks, those piercing eyes that remind me of ebony leave a trail of heat as he drifts them from my feet up to my chest. Once he reaches my eyes, a smirk lifts the corner of his mouth. "Come here, *Bella*," he commands.

When this Lucio Russo enters the room, my world spins on its axis. Air gets sucked out because he commands it. There's confidence oozing from him, dark and dangerous.

"Strip for me. I'll watch." Once again, it's an order, not a request. The chair I was sitting on only moments ago is where he sits, his legs spread as he watches me with those dark eyes. Tentatively, I reach for the hem of my tank top, tugging it in a slow movement up my torso until it's lying in a heap at his shoes.

Silence hangs heavy around us, but as he shifts in the seat, I notice the gun peeking out from his jacket. Fear skyrockets my heart rate and I wonder why he's wearing it inside the house. I've never seen it before.

"Is something wrong, Bella?" His question startles me out of my thoughts. When he notices where my line of sight is glued, he leans forward, his elbows on his knees. "Are you afraid of me?" The smirk on his face tells me it doesn't bother him in the slightest if I am. Perhaps he wants me to be scared.

"Why would I be?"

"Because I'm a wicked man, Raina," he warns, as he does every time we're together, but each time, I want him more.

"You say that, but you've never shown me."

Suddenly, he pushes off the chair and stalks toward me with a plan dancing in his eyes. Instinctively, I back away, my gaze locked on his. In two long strides, he reaches me and leans in with his face inches from mine. I move back instinctively as he closes the distance. Seconds later, my back hits the wall, and I realize I have nowhere to go. There is no escape, and I'm alone at home because

Lucio broke in. He leans in, his body pressed against mine.

The heat of his breath warms me. The way his chest rises and falls in the expensive suit makes me want to touch him, but I know I shouldn't. Maybe all this time I've been playing with fire and I'm about to get burned. "Take off your clothes, all of them. Now," he bites out almost angrily, but I recognize the desire swimming in his dark eyes.

I make quick work of ridding myself of my shorts, panties, and I unclasp my bra that's molded to my full breasts. He shrugs off his jacket, throwing it on my bed before he reaches for his gun. My breathing hitches in my throat. My heart thuds wildly against my ribs.

One of his large hands finds my hip, resting firmly yet gently on it, which only serves to scorch my skin from his touch. "I'll show you what wicked men do to little girls who want to play with them," he murmurs, almost as if he's cooing a baby to sleep. "You've done things to me, sweet girl, so many things you shouldn't have. Four long years and all I want is you." The cold metal of the weapon trails from my cheek, down my neck, sending a cool shiver down my spine.

"What things, Lucio?" My voice is merely a whisper, nothing more than a needy whimper that makes him smile. He's tall, dark, and handsome, but so beautifully scary, that it makes me quiver.

I know nothing of guns, so I do not know if it's loaded or ready to fire. The barrel inches its way between my breasts, easily finding my belly button moments later. I think he's going to stop, but he doesn't. Instead, he slips the cold steel between my thighs. A gasp, loud and filled with shock, falls from my lips.

"Do you feel that, Bella?" The way his head tips to the side as he regards me makes him look evil, sinister. "Open your legs." The deep growl of his voice sends heat coursing through me.

"Please, Lucio." My whimper is rough with fear, need, and lust. I have no choice because each moment this man comes near me, I can't fight him off. It's as if I'm addicted to him. I crave him. He's a drug, and I'm an addict.

"Do it!" he bites out and I obey swiftly. He nudges my pussy and I know I'm drenched.

Does fear turn me on? Yes. *Am I fucking crazy?* Probably. But the metal barrel slides into my core easily as he fucks me with his gun.

My head drops back, my mouth falls open on a pleasured moan, and my fingers grip the wall behind me. Digging my nails into the concrete, I try to find purchase on something, but I can't. My knees shake. My thighs tremble as this man, this very dangerous criminal, fucks me with his gun. He moves slowly at first, but then the movements speed up. Goose bumps rise on every inch of my skin from the motions.

Lucio leans in close, his lips at my ear when he orders in a low, feral growl, "Come for me, Raina. Come on my gun inside your cunt."

My world explodes in that second. My toes curl into the carpet and his arm bands around my waist as I drench his weapon with my juices. Suddenly, the gun is wrenched from me and I'm impaled on his cock. Thick and hard, it hits me in *that* spot and I see stars. I feel the cool metal on my mouth as he paints my lips with the arousal on his gun.

His hips move against me, pinning me hard against the wall. My legs wrap easily around his middle, pulling him in deeper, needing more of him. His mouth finds purchase on my neck as he suckles the flesh into his mouth.

His teeth bear down on my skin, and I know he's marking me. A feeling niggles in my chest, a sadness or fear,

I'm not sure what, but I can't comprehend what it is because he's moving inside me, giving me the connection I wanted.

He sucks hard on my neck, his teeth breaking skin, and I know he's drawing blood. Another orgasm slams into me and I bite down on my lower lip until I taste blood. He continues to fuck me relentlessly, faster and faster, as his hips slam me into the wall. A second later, his body locks. A groan rumbles in his chest as he fills me with his seed.

"Good girl," he murmurs.

And that's when he leaves me in my bedroom, alone, shocked, and sated.

3

FRANCO

Four of my men stalk inside the office first.

Once it's swept for any hiding enemies, I enter with my two brothers. Lucio told me to wait. Once his call came through twenty minutes ago to confirm he'd finished the meeting he was attending, I made my move. The thing is, his message was garbled with random mumbling, which made no sense. My gut churns with worry when I think about his ragged plea—*get here now*. It's not like him to ask for help, but when he did, I heard the agony in his tone.

My one bodyguard, Enrico, saunters toward me, holding out a folder. It's thick, bound with the crimson ribbon my father used to use on all his official paperwork. He'd bind it in such a way that would ensure nobody could open it and reseal it. And now, my cousin has done the same, which only strengthens the feeling of dread that's settled in my chest.

"Where did you find this?" I question.

"Sir," Enrico mutters, "it was as you said, in the drawer, but..." his words taper off to nothing, causing me to glance at him. His gaze drops to the floor, which sets me on alert.

"I think you may want to see this," he tells me, turning and heading deeper into the office. Our footfalls are the only sound in the room.

When we reach the bookshelves, I notice they're shoved aside. Someone found Lucio's hidden room. I enter without concern for everyone else. I know what I'll find. It's been clawing at me since my phone call.

As soon as I step inside the hidden room, I feel red-hot rage course through my veins. I scrunched the folder in my hand as violence niggles at me, pushing and pulling at my mind. Revenge. Lucio's body is draped in the chair as if he'd fallen asleep.

But he's not sleeping.

His head is twisted obscenely. Blood has seeped through his crisp white shirt, and the mark of our enemy is carved on his forehead. But it's not only my cousin who sits in this room, murdered. There's another man, older, who has had his throat sliced open, his head barely hanging on by the spine attaching it to the rest of his body.

"Who the fuck is that?"

"We don't know yet, sir," Enrico informs me. "We've got Gian coming in to do a sweep of the scene before we get cleanup in here."

Nodding, I blink away the red spots of rage that blind me as I spin on my heel and shove by the men who followed me into the chamber of horrors. I ignore my brothers calling to me as I make my way toward the exit. I need fresh air. If I don't breathe, I'll go on a killing rampage without asking questions. That's not how I was taught.

My father was always precise in his vengeance.

And I will be too.

I slip into the car and tug the knot from the ribbon, causing the blood-red material to fall to the floor. Opening the folder, I scan the first page. It's a letter addressed to me, from Lucio, explaining the evidence he found where the Santillo family are broaching on our territory. He found a mole who's been feeding the assholes information about us.

I'm livid by the time I get near the end of his letter, but the last part stops me in my tracks.

Since you're reading this, I have finally met our maker. So, there's something I need your help with, cugino. It will destroy something delicate and precious to me when she learns of my death. I need you to go to her, to Raina Lombardi. Take her and keep her safe from the wrath that will soon fall on her. She's too innocent for this life to be dragged into it.

I've never asked you for much, Franco. But... I loved her. She was my heart, my soul. And because of our blood line, I can't be there to keep her safe. So, it falls to you. You're in charge, and I'd not trust anyone else with her.

She's alone in this world now. Her brother, Andrea, he's bad news. You need to get her away from him as soon as possible. He's fallen in with the Santillos and there's no telling what he'll do. Please. I beg of you, cugino.

Questo è tutto ciò che ti chiedo. This is all I ask of you.

My hands are shaking with frustration, anger, and sadness. He wants me to fucking babysit his girlfriend. As irritated as I am at his letter, I know I can never deny his last request. He's putting me in a position I shouldn't be in. There's a reason I don't have a woman on my arm. This life isn't made for loving marriages or relationships. This is an existence of bloodshed and pain.

The car door opens and my brothers slip in, not long after we're joined by our driver.

"And?" Matteo questions, his eyes glued to mine.

"We need to take down the Santillos. They're responsible for the death of our cousin."

Gio rubs his hands together as if I've told him we're off on a month-long beach vacation. That's the one thing about my brother, also well known as The Player. He is excited about jobs that we do, but killing isn't his forte. As the nickname suggests, he loves to play with his food before he makes the kill.

"I'm ready," Matteo offers.

"So am I." Gio smirks.

4

RAINA

I'm still shaking. My body was long overdue to rest. Last night, my childhood home went up in flames and I don't know who did it. I don't know who I can set out to claim my revenge from because I didn't see the men who ransacked the house.

When I heard a noise downstairs, I didn't investigate. I did what my father always taught me to. I hid in my closet until silence greeted me. Then I smelled the burning. It slowly traveled upstairs and soon I was sputtering and choking.

Thankfully, Daddy had the insight to build me a small balcony and staircase that led down to the garden of our home. The police and fire department arrived, along with Andrea. My life blew up in a pile of rubble as I watched.

Daddy didn't come home, so I waited up most of the night. As much as I know he said he'd be okay, I have a bad feeling about the meeting he was heading to. This life is dangerous, I know it is, and something tells me that if he doesn't call soon, something far worse than a general meeting has taken place.

As soon as the police arrived, they'd asked me questions, but I said nothing about where my father had gone or what he was doing. All they know is that he's away on business. My mother hasn't been answering her phone, and I'm stuck here with my brother, who I hate.

Secrets and lies are something that run rampant in my family. With my father gone, my mother off the grid, and only me and Andrea here, I have to help him run the club.

My father didn't want me in this life, but since I turned eighteen, Daddy allowed me to work at Gin Bar. It was a gift to my brother from our father. With each hour that passes today, I have a strange feeling that I'll soon be under the care of Andrea, and that fills me with dread.

If something really has happened to Dad, I know what his Will and Testament would read, and that makes me want to cry. I thought I'd be able to escape this life. To run away from my brother with *him*. But I don't see how that can happen. Lucio and my father's disappearance have involuntarily dragged me into it.

Lucio's phone has been off since yesterday. After he left, he sent me one last text message and when I tried calling back, the phone rang directly to his voice mail. I've read it a few hundred times, trying to make sense of it, and as much as I've tried to decode it, I can't.

Life has a funny way of fucking with you when you least expect it. I wanted a different life, but with Andrea controlling everything, I'll merely be a prisoner. I thought my dark prince would take me away with him. He promised.

I pull my hair from the elastic band and breathe a long sigh of relief. My body aches from the treadmill, but my heart pains for another reason. For the one thing I'll never have—my freedom.

My best friend flops onto the chair in my new bedroom and regards me. I met Adria at school. We were in our first year of high school when we found kinship with each other.

She was fiery, more so than I ever could be. Even though she pushes me to speak up, to speak out, I am not like her. She's been my only salvation while living under the constant surveillance of Dad and the men I know he has following me around.

She watches me for a long while, and I know she wants to talk about what happened. About the new home I have. Andrea put down a deposit on a furnished apartment close to town and told me to stay put. Unless I'm at work or the gym, I'm not to go anywhere.

The man my brother decided to be my shadow has been glued to my ass for the past eight hours and it's frustrating. I've never had to deal with this side of the life, but now that it's been thrust onto me, I decide I don't like it one bit.

"I can't believe the entire house is gone." Adria's words make me sad. They remind me of all the memories I've lost. Except one thing. The only thing I have are the photos of Lucio. Those I stole from Daddy's office when I was rummaging around in his paperwork.

"I guess my father must have royally pissed someone off," I tell her.

Adria doesn't know everything about our lineage. She knows we're Italian, but our connection to the mafia has never come up and if she doesn't ask, I don't offer. We've only known each other for a couple of years, but I've always kept secrets. Like I said, the Lombardi name is well known for its hidden truths and wicked sins.

She bought the story that my father's clients are politicians, well-known people with connections. I told a lie. A little one, but it was something I had to come up with, so she wouldn't suspect me of being part of a crime family. Also, she's never met my boyfriend. At least, that's what I think of him as. I don't know what he is to me officially, but I could never tell her I'm with Lucio Russo.

When I turn to face her, my best friend stares at me in disbelief, but I shrug, attempting to calm the agony that's gripped my heart since the flames stole everything.

"I'm so sorry, Rai." She pouts. Adria is incredibly beautiful. Her long dark hair is shiny and sleek, her eyes are almost feline, the color of honey, and her lips—full and always bright red.

She never talks about her family, but I know she hides secrets just like me. Like everyone in my life does, including Lucio. Her father is notorious in Los Angeles for violence and I've heard about the people he's hurt who double-crossed him. Something tells me he'll not think twice about killing a man.

If only my dark prince would save me from this life, I'd take Adria with me and we'd be free. My sour thoughts disappear when my best friend shakes me from the dreams that will now be nothing but a young girl's wishes.

"I just have to start fresh." I attempt a cheerful response as I stalk into the kitchen, allowing her to follow me. She walks over to the countertop to pour boiling water into the mug I set out earlier. My favorite. Tea. It always seems to calm me down. "I mean... Andrea is looking for the culprits, and the police will arrest them, and it will be fine." I shrug, making sure my fabrication is as believable as I can make it out to be because deep down I know the law will never be involved.

"If you want me to stay with you,"—she drags the words out on a sigh—"I can keep you company, cheer you up, until you find some hottie to do that for you." She waggles her brows dramatically.

I know she's trying to help, but it's not. Thoughts of Lucio and the last time we were together burn in my mind.

"I better get ready for work. I can't afford to get on my brother's bad side this early on my shift," I inform Adri.

She grabs her purse and heads for the door but stops to turn to me. "I'll be around later. Maybe we can eat ice cream and drink cheap wine." Adria smiles. I know she's trying to make me feel better, and I smile, attempting to look normal with everything that's happened.

"Sounds good. Thanks, Adri."

She leaves, and I head into my bedroom and flop onto the bed. I need a long shower. Hopefully, it will calm my muscles and my tumbling thoughts. Pulling my phone from my purse, I glance at the time and note that I've got an hour to get ready.

Living in Los Angeles had its perks. There are the beautiful beaches, Napa Valley just up the road, but there is a dark side that nobody knows about. The side where I spend every day earning a living. The Gin Bar was every bit as elite as its competition. Decked in black and silver, it had been in my family for many years, from my grandfather to my father, and then on to my brother. He's the owner, and he never allows me to forget it.

I try my father's phone again, but it goes directly to voicemail. Leaving a message for him to call me urgently, I know he won't get it. Right down to my soul, I know my father is no longer living. There isn't any proof, no body to mourn over, but I have a feeling that even when we find him, he'll not be able to give me that smile that would always set my nightmares to sleep.

I head in the bathroom and turn on the shower. Stripping down, I step inside and allow my mind to flit to Lucio. To the moment we first met, to the time he walked out of my bedroom only twenty-four hours ago.

He gave me all I needed in a partner. No promises of forever—at least, none that he voiced—just good sex. He preferred it rough. And as a brutal man in business, he was a fierce man in bed. My body hungered for what he gave.

With those thoughts weighing heavily on my mind, I lather up, massaging my tired thighs and calves. Working in the bar takes strain on my feet and legs, on top of the ten miles I ran today, and all I'll want after my shift will be my bed. Unfortunately, my brother is as strict with me as if I were any employee in his bar and if he feels like having a late one with friends, I'll have to work.

He's always been different, a little more volatile, and I would imagine him being adopted. Not of the Lombardi bloodline because my father was stringent, but he was never an asshole.

Growing up with an older brother wasn't easy, but with Andrea now an adult, he's made life even more difficult. Once I rinse my hair, I step out of the shower and wrap myself in a fluffy white towel. In my bedroom, a light vibration comes from my bed, and when I pick up my phone, I see Lucio's name flash on the screen.

"Hello?" I answer quickly, but I'm met with silence. "Hello? Is anyone there?" My chest tightens and my heart thuds against my ribs. "Lucio?" Seconds later, he hangs up. I set the device down, but as I do, another buzz comes through. This time it's not a call, but a message.

Time has run out, little princess.

My heart rate spikes, threatening to choke me. I respond immediately, asking what he means. A gut feeling tells me this isn't the man I've known since I was fifteen. This isn't Lucio.

Game over.

· · ·

The loud ringing of the tone I set for Andrea screeches at me, causing me to squeal. I swipe my finger over the screen and press the phone to my ear.

"Get to the bar now. Something's happened."

He hangs up before I have time to respond. This time, when I try to swallow, I can't. My body shivers with confusion, with fear, and the anxiety tightens my belly. I race to my closet and grab my uniform. A black knee-length skirt with ballet flats and a charcoal, silk blouse. I quickly towel dry my hair until it's damp, hanging in long honey-colored waves down my back.

Not bothering with makeup, I rush into the living room, grab my keys, and head for the door. It's still warm outside and as I lock up, I take a deep breath. The sun is setting on the horizon, casting everything in a deep orange glow. The secondhand electric-blue Audi my father bought me when I turned seventeen is my only possession I have left of him. All the photos, gifts, teddy bears, it all went up in smoke when they burned our home to the ground.

I don't focus on the road. My mind is running a million miles a minute with scenarios. I wish Andrea had just told me what happened, but of course he needs the control. He loves to watch my panic, my pain. My brother has become my worst enemy, even though he's my greatest ally.

Pulling into the parking lot, I turn off the engine, open my door, and grab my purse. Inhaling a deep breath, I exit the car and lock it.

"Raina." My brother's thick drawl drags my attention to the garage door where he's leaning against the steel with a cigarette hanging from his lips.

Dressed in a black Cartier suit with a crisp blue button-up and a charcoal tie. His shoes are shiny in the low light.

Girls compare him to James Dean, with those blue-green eyes and that sleek, tousled hair with a cheeky grin. A bad boy from a young age, he's always done what he wanted, but since he got into the wrong crowd, it was as if a switch had turned on inside him and he became a bigger asshole than he always had been.

"Andrea, what's going on?" My response earns me a dark chuckle. I don't need to cast a glance at my watch, knowing I've arrived exactly on time.

"Dear old Dad has kicked the bucket," he utters the words casually, as if he's telling me the sun is shining.

"What?" I croak, emotion thick in my tone. Tears brim my eyes and Andrea looks blurry suddenly. "What do you mean?"

"I've just gotten confirmation that Dad was murdered. I am now in charge of *everything.*" The way he says it explains just what I believed he'd do. He means he's in charge of me. "I've got an important meeting tonight, some big players coming in. I want you to serve us in the VIP lounge." He pulls on the white stick and blows out a billow of gray smoke.

"You've just told me our father is dead," I retort, but all I earn myself is a grin. *Asshole.*

"I know, and I've just told you I am in charge. If you don't get your ass in there and serve drinks, I'll be forced to disown you. And you will lose everything." The threat burns through me. My hand rears back, and it makes quick contact with his face.

Andrea chortles, a low rumble from his chest, and I note there is a cut on his lip. I've drawn blood from my own brother. He slides his palm over his cheek, regarding me with a tipped head and narrowed eyes.

"Try that again, little sister"—he sneers, leaning in so his breath is on me—"and I'll make you rue the day you were born. I am your guardian in every sense of the word, and make no mistake, I'll be setting some new rules." By that I know he means the trust fund our father had in place. Dad didn't keep it a secret that he had set one up for me. Andrea got his when he turned twenty-four, and I'll only receive mine at the same age. Sadness washes over me when the realization hits that I'll be Andrea's slave for another five long years.

"Fuck you!" I bite out, reaching out to slap him once more, but he's too fast this time. He grips my hand, holding on to my wrist painfully. The venom in his eyes is volatile, and it scares me. Yes, he's never been a good brother, but something has changed, something drastic.

"Watch your tongue, little sister. These men might just like your little virgin act you've got going. Perhaps they'll do all that shit you like to read about in your smutty books you love so much." He smirks, falling into step beside me as he practically drags me into the building.

"Why are you doing this? Daddy would never have wanted you to turn into *them*," I retort, changing the subject, trying to level with him, but he doesn't relent. My brother found one of my novels one day while rifling through my purse for something. To this day, I never found out what he was searching for and when I asked, he dismissed it as a trivial act.

"Daddy's no longer here. Now get to work," he bites out in amusement before leaving me in the main area and disappearing into the office.

The interior of the club is decked out in monotones, with the only color being some of our waitresses' hair. Our uniforms are mostly black and silver, keeping the theme minimal, but even with the elegance of the furnishings, there's an underlying current of depravity that happens behind the scenes.

My thoughts are searing through me. *Daddy's dead.* That's when I recall the message from Lucio's phone. *Game over.*

Did he kill my father?

It makes little sense. He had no reason to. They both worked for the same organization. The Cosa Nostra. All I want is to get out of this place, to mourn the loss of not only my home, but my father, too. The tears fall when I blink.

I'm numb. I can't feel anything. Grabbing a crystal tumbler, I quickly pour a double shot of the whiskey my brother always drinks, and I swallow it in one long gulp. The burn causes me to choke. Coughing and spluttering, I race for the tap and fill the glass with water. The cool liquid eases the burn in my throat and I fill it once more.

"Hey, Raina." Giulia's excitable tone comes from behind the sleek silver bar. She's the loud, overly confident girl out of all our staff, always dressed in designer jeans and exquisite blouses. Now that I take her in, though, it seems she's either become less concerned with the expensive clothes and more about functionality, or there's another reason for her dressed as if she'd just rolled out of bed.

"You look..."

"Yeah, don't ask. Asshole of a boyfriend dumped me out of the apartment, so I've been sleeping on a friend's sofa." She huffs, stalking by me and into the staff room behind the bar.

I take in the bar, leaving her to change, and notice it's slowly filling up with after work clients. Men in expensive tailor-made suits and briefcases that could probably hold a lot of money or weapons. Knowing the normal caliber of clientele, I'd say both apply.

When Giulia reappears, I take in her appearance now. I can't help noticing she's dressed in the tightest damn tank top I've ever seen, shimmery and silver. She looks like she's going out clubbing instead of serving high-end liquor to men old enough to be our father.

"What the hell are you wearing?" I hiss as she nears me.

"A top. One that will earn me a lot of tips." She smirks, winking with that cheekiness that always gets her into trouble. Shaking my head, I head to the small staff room and drop my purse in the safe. When I enter the main bar area again I grab the tray of glasses, setting them on the countertop, ready for the shift. "You should try it some time. Maybe you'll find a rich man to fuck that uptight ass of yours."

"Do you have to be a bitch?" I bite out my response. Her eyes widen in shock. We've always joked around, but today is not the day for it. "I'm sorry. I've just gotten some devastating news."

"Are you okay?" she murmurs, holding my arms, attempting to meet my watery gaze.

Nodding, I sniffle. "My dad," is all I get out before I finally break. My body is wracked with sobs. She pulls me into her arms, keeping me close while I cry. And cry I do. The pain finally searing through everything and I'm lost to it. I can't let Andrea see me like this. He'll lose his shit.

I pull away, attempting to calm myself. Sobs still wrack my body and Giulia offers me a solemn smile.

"Why don't you freshen up." Her gaze darts to the office door and I know she's as worried about Andrea hearing us or seeing me in this state.

I leave her behind the bar. The ladies' room is quiet when I step inside, and I splash my face with water, attempting to calm the puffiness from crying. "I miss you, Daddy."

Shaking my head, I straighten my spine, remembering what he would always tell me.

Strength comes from within. Not a name. Not a family. But

from your soul. Nobody has the same one. Some are dark. Some light. But you, my sweet girl, you're my star in the night.

Even though it's getting busier in the bar when I make my way back to work, I take my place behind the counter, my white apron tied around my slim hips.

I pour drinks. I ignore the jibes from drunk assholes.

"You okay?" Giulia questions an hour later.

I nod.

I swallow.

I turn away.

"You need a night of debauchery." She smiles, her whisper clearly loud enough to bring attention to us from one gentleman who's sitting at the bar. His cool gaze drinks her in and his lips lift into a smirk.

"I'm sure I could oblige you, sweet thing," he purrs, a deep, seductive tone that has me rolling my eyes. Men like this are bad news. They're old enough to be my father. The thought chokes me.

"Why don't you leave me a tip, and we'll see." She giggles, trying to bring attention to herself instead of me. The girl who's about to break down.

Even though she's right, I'd love to experience having a normal life. Being able to go out, get drunk, dance the night away, but I'm not normal. I never will be. Also, I'm not that type of girl. Lucio had ensured I was safe, never out of my home or his sight. When I was with him, I was in a type of prison. But I grew up in one, so I never knew the difference.

"What about you, Poppet?" he murmurs at me as he lifts his chin in a gesture, but before I can respond, an accented voice that's as smoky as the most expensive Scotch whisky and as deep as a baritone rumbles behind me.

"She's busy tonight." The words sound around me, as if they're caressing me, stroking me in places I ache to be touched. When I turn to regard my savior, my voice is stolen along with my body.

He's beautiful. Handsome.

With day-old stubble that covers his square jawline, sharp features, and piercing black eyes he holds me hostage with a stare that's hot enough to disintegrate my panties.

His mouth looks as sinful as a decadent dessert. But there's a dangerous aura that seems to waft from him. A sleek jet-black Armani suit which encompasses his broad shoulders. His dress shirt is a deep red, which looks almost black in the low lights of the bar. The silver tie is shiny and pops starkly against the darkness. Tanned skin with that accent tells me he's Italian. I've spent my young life around men like him, with the men who could have killed my father.

His short black hair is styled in a messy way, as if he's run his fingers through it a few times. Or he's had some woman's hands tugging at the strands while he buried his face between her thighs as his sinful mouth devoured her. The thought has me squirming involuntarily.

"Can…" Clearing my throat, I try again. "Can I get you anything?" My meek voice makes me sound like a child or a mouse. *Jesus, get a grip.* His gaze travels with such slow precision from my feet, up my legs and torso, only stopping momentarily on my chest, and he drags his dark piercing stare to my sky-blue eyes. Every moment his eyes are on me, my skin tingles. It feels like a match has been struck and I'm about to burst into flames.

"A bottle of the Balvenie Scotch, fifty-year-old, and three tumblers. Bring it to The Lounge." With that, he turns and walks away without so much as a glance behind him.

My eyes don't want to look away. As if he's the glue and I'm the paper. He must be the most devilishly striking man I've ever seen, besides Lucio. Turning to get the order, I grab three crystal glasses and place them on the tray, along with the whisky he's requested.

My hands tremble and I fight to calm the need that's coiled in my belly. Oh, the sinful things I'm sure he can do. That I want him to do. *Calm your shit down, Raina.*

In that moment, he reminds me of Lucio. How he commanded a room when he entered. How as soon as he opened his mouth, people would flee or come closer. And my heart aches. It thuds painfully, reminding me I've lost two men I love. My father, certainly dead. But the man who's offered me a new lease on life has just disappeared.

The stranger is gone, but his presence lingers. Something about him seemed familiar. Like he knew me. My body trickles with confused emotions warring inside me and all he did was look at me.

Jesus, imagine if he touched me.

5
FRANCO

"Mr. Moretti, it's good to see you. Please, have a seat." Andrea Lombardi is an asshole, and it takes all of my restraint not to kill him right here and now. I know he has connections to who killed Lucio. His name came up a few times in our findings, so here I am, dealing with an asshole. This prissy piece of shit is one I'd rather do without, but I set my mind on vengeance.

His sister was the girl Lucio told me about. In his letter, he mentioned Raina Lombardi. I have to keep her safe, to fucking babysit. As much as I wanted to refuse, I can't. He's my blood and there's nothing that will make me reject his dying wish.

"Mr. Lombardi, I'm sure you know why I've asked for this meeting," I respond as I unbutton my suit jacket and settle in the expensive leather seat. I wanted to kidnap Raina, to lock her away in my house, but I know I'll have this asshole to deal with.

He follows suit, sitting opposite me with a shit-eating grin on his face that I'd like to wipe off with my fist. Before he can respond, the door swings open and my brothers saunter in. Giovanni and Matteo couldn't be more different if they tried. Both in looks and personality, but there's one thing they do well, and that's kill. Especially assholes like this.

"Sorry we're late. There was a problem," Matteo murmurs but offers nothing more. Once they're seated, the door glides open and I know who it is before she enters. The woman who caught my eye, but she's Lucio's. Or was rather. That thought sours my mood as soon as it flits through my mind.

Carrying a silver tray with three tumblers and a bottle of the whisky I asked for, she's dressed in a demure outfit and a pair of ballet shoes. Even though she's young, far too young, I can't help assessing her. My cousin had good taste in women.

Her body is curvy—soft and pliable. Her skin is creamy with a soft blush on her cheeks. I can easily imagine her in my bedroom, on her knees with those doe eyes peering up at me as she begs for me to teach her how to swallow my cock. How I'd love to show her how much of a villain I can be. To mark her creamy skin with the palm of my hand or my belt.

"Brother." Turning to Gio, I glance at the smirk on his face and shake my head. This is a job. She's not mine. I shouldn't be thinking about her in that way. My cousin would've had my balls if I went near her.

"Is there anything else?" Her soft-spoken question has me flitting my dark stare on her. She's watching my intently. *Do I remind her of her lost lover? Does she know he's dead?*

"That's all, thank you," I respond, my tone firm and commanding. Testing her.

A simple smile crosses her features and she gives me a curt nod. Her hair is golden brown—which hangs in soft waves to the middle of her back—a hint darker than blond. Blue eyes that remind me of the ocean—the translucent sea of Reggio Calabria, of home—pin me with a questioning gaze. It's as if she's trying to read me.

My gaze drops to her chest, taking in her ample breasts. Even though they're not overly visible in the blouse she wears, I know they'd fit perfectly in my hands. It's enough to taunt me from the soft silk that hides them from my gaze. I wonder if her nipples are sensitive. She's distracting me from business, which isn't good, but there's something about her, as if she wants the danger. Perhaps that was her reasoning behind dating Lucio.

"Let's get this meeting started. Thank you, Raina, you can leave now," Andrea grunts out rudely, and she merely nods. The way he treats her angers me. If I had my way, I'd gut the fucker right now. How I'd revel in watching him bleed out.

I grab the tumbler and drain it of the amber liquid, savoring the burn. "There have been two murders in the city. As I'm sure you are aware, we don't take kindly to people encroaching on our territory. Your name," I tell him as I pour another three-finger shot, then continue once I lift the tumbler toward my mouth, "has come up a few times."

"I can assure you, Mr. Moretti, I have heard nothing about this."

"So you don't know your father was killed?" My question stills him for a moment, shock clear on his face, and I know he's hiding something. His eyes, they tell me what I need to know. He's in on this. I'm not sure how, but I'll find out.

"I-I got the call this morning," he stutters, shifting in his seat.

"And you're not the least bit concerned about who did

it?" I take a swallow of my drink, watching him, assessing him, reading every nuance of the lying bastard.

He clears his throat, ready to spew a lie. "Of course I am, I just haven't had time to take it all in." I'm surprised he even had the balls to sound like he's saddened. Unfortunately, his acting abilities aren't up to par.

"I will work my way through the organizations as I focus on finding my cousin's and your father's murderer." Another gulp and my glass is empty. "I trust I'll have your support when I need your paperwork?"

"I have little left. Our family home burned to the ground only a day ago."

I know this already, but I wanted to see his reaction to it. Far too casual. As if it's not fazed him, he lost everything.

"That's tragic," I tell him, leaning back, my one ankle resting on my opposite thigh.

"It was," he says. His eyes land on the weapon in the holster. I know my jacket has opened enough to show him I'm armed, and I'm ready to take him out if need be.

"If you don't get me the information I request, we'll need to remove you, whatever your family has left from our books."

The asshole's eyes widen as he stutters in fear of losing the bar, along with a few hundred million. Much to Matteo's and Gio's amusement, who know exactly what would happen if he were to fuck this up.

"No, no, there's no need to do that. I've got the documents my father held at his home office on file. We backed up everything last year to our online systems. They're all secure. Take this." He gestures to a small USB flash drive in his hand, which could never hold what I need.

He's a little boy playing big boys games, and there's only one thing that happens to assholes like that. They get bled out over the edge of a pier and dumped into the depths.

"Then this meeting is done, Andrea." I watch him for a moment, then offer a smirk. "Gio, grab the damn thing. I have better things to do than sit here. If we need anything more..." I allow my words to taper off in warning.

As soon as my little brother rises, Andrea grips the USB, meeting my glare.

"I'll have it ready."

Before he has time to take a fucking breath between words, I've stood up and pulled my custom Glock from the holster hidden by my jacket. I point it at the fucker, unlocking the safety. Ice-cold fear flits across his face and I can't help smirking. Pinning him with a glare, I demand, "This is not a fucking game, Mr. Lombardi. I suggest you remember I can end you. I can end everything you stand for, and I won't even think twice about doing it." The fiery bite in my tone is nothing short of commanding, and I'm sure the little boy has pissed himself because I stalk forward, holding the gun on him, aiming the short barrel between his dark eyes.

"I'd listen to Franco. He's crazy, and he's definitely not afraid of spilling blood." Matteo steps forward. When I cast a quick glance at my brother, he's got his blade out, swishing it back and forth between his fingers. He's known for carving pieces of shit like this into works of art and if I let him loose right now, Mr. Lombardi will be ribbons of flesh in no time.

"Fine. Yes, anything you need. I'll do anything you ask. I'm innocent in all this." He watches me, but I don't respond. Like fuck he's innocent. There's only one way he'll gain my trust, and it won't be in this life.

Shouldering my gun, I pick up the bottle of whisky and pour a double shot into the tumbler. As I lift the glass to my lips, Gio grabs the flash drive and I swallow the shot in one long gulp. "It was good doing business with you, Mr. Lombardi. I'll see you soon." With that, I turn on my heel and walk out of the lounge.

As soon as I get home, I'll be scouring the information. I have two men working around the clock to get meetings with all my Captains. Once I've met with each one, those who've gone rogue will be dealt with.

I wonder if it's time to make a call. Since Lucio's demise, I've been putting it off. But I know it's wrong of me to do so. I should've called him yesterday. When I get to my office, I'll do it. I'll have to call Luciano, Lucio's older brother. The two of them used to be thick as thieves until the falling-out. I haven't spoken to Luciano in years. Mainly because we hate each other.

Stepping into the bar, I find her behind the counter, wiping the smooth silver surface. Her hair is wavier now, almost curly. Those inquisitive eyes peek up as soon as I am near her. The pain in them is palpable. She's lost far too much. And I'll ensure she loses nothing else. A small, sad smile curls her perfect, plump lips. She's enticing, a seductive tease. I wonder if she realizes how much power she wields with a simple smile.

"Raina, is it?" I question, tipping my head to the side as I regard her.

"Yes, sir." Two words that do things to me, things I shouldn't want. I was only supposed to make sure she's safe, but there's an underlying sadness and wariness that burns in her eyes. A spark of recognition that she understands who I am and what I do.

My promise was to find her and make sure she was away from her asshole brother, but one look at her, and I've changed the vow I made to a dying man. I want her and there's no way she's going to get away from me. A niggling deep in my gut tells me to steal her away. I can easily have her on a jet in an hour on the way to Europe where her asshole brother will never see her again. Sadly, I can't do that because my business here is far from over.

"Are you working tomorrow night?"

She nods, placing the glass on the counter and giving me her undivided attention. *Good girl.* I want to murmur the words but don't. Instead, I smile. Silent and predatory. An expert hunter always learns about his prey before he pounces. Before he attacks and viciously devours every morsel of sinful flesh. And when I get her on her back, she'll be begging for more. *I'm sorry, Lucio. You gave her to me. Now there's no turning back.*

"Good, I'll see you tomorrow, Raina."

Before she can respond, I'm sauntering out the door with my brothers a step behind.

"Are you sure that's a good idea, Franco? She's... *allettante.* So fucking tempting," Gio murmurs as we head toward my town car. She is enticing.

"He asked me to watch her. That's what I'm doing," I respond, sliding into the bench seat of the black SUV. Once Gio and Matteo are seated, Lorenzo, our driver, pulls away and the farther away we get, the appeal to go back in there becomes stronger. Perhaps my little brother is right. This might not be a good idea. But I'm fucked because I can't walk away.

"Watching differs from what I can see racing through your mind," Mateo offers. He's right. He knows me too well. She's far too young and off-limits. But then again, when did I ever limit myself when I wanted something?

"Perhaps," I tell him.

"She's only nineteen, Franco," Gio hisses, almost angrily. But I know he's more concerned than angry. His eyes glower at me, matching my glare with one of his own.

"She is," I concede. "But Lucio asked something of me he knew I could never deny. And if a gift is handed to you on a silver platter, do you refuse it?"

"She's not an object."

"Matteo, are you really judging me by this choice?" I question him incredulously. Leaning forward, I place my elbows on my thighs, meeting my brother's eyes.

"No, just..." He sighs. "Be careful with her."

I nod, sitting back, and silence envelops us easily. My mind still racing with thoughts of her. It's wrong. So fucking wrong. But I don't care. I never did, and I never will.

Raina Lombardi will be mine.

***

"This is why I asked you to fucking do it last night!" I slam down the phone in frustration. Pinning Gio with a glare, I bite out, "Get the fuck outside with that damn thing." He's smoking in my office again and he knows I fucking hate it.

"*Gesù, clamati.*" He chuckles, rising from the chair. With a confident stride, he heads to the balcony that sits just off my large office and pushes open the glass doors. Light and fresh air stream through the room, bathing the space in a false serenity.

"Don't fucking tell me to calm down. Do you know how much money was lost? *Che stronzo!* The asshole didn't follow orders."

Giovanni doesn't respond. Instead, he puffs the white smoke into the clean air outside. Matteo shifts in his seat, lifting the laptop, and places it on my desk. "This is what you're looking for." He points to the information I've been waiting for.

The background intel on Raina Lombardi.

Just as I figured—no siblings. So how is it that Andrea

has claim to the money and is titled as her brother? When I got home last night, I did some research into the Lombardis. They only had one child. My men who scrape the dark web for anything I need to bring my enemies down found out that she's the only child, heir to the fortune.

Did Lucio know this? There wasn't anything in the file he left behind.

Her father was murdered and her mother is gone. Disappeared. Raina's single. She's nineteen, turning twenty in a few months, and she's applied to study at Princeton. She wants to go into finance, like her father. Everything is there, blood type, all known addresses, even the type of contraceptive she's on.

"Do you think you should do this?" Giovanni questions from the doorway, the sunlight stealing his features, his face half in shadow as he regards me with narrowed eyes. He might be younger than me and I know he's only trying to be the voice of reason, but I've made my decision. There's nothing and nobody that's going to stop me from having her.

"An opportunity had landed in my lap. I'm not letting slip through my fingers. Let's see if her brother can handle my games. He wants to fuck with *la mafia*, I'll teach him how the big boys play. There's something he's hiding, and if my gut feeling is right, he was the one who killed Lucio. Like the saying goes, an eye for an eye. This time, however, it will be a life for a life." I flit my gaze between them. Both nod quickly. They know the life. They know that soon, we'll need to avenge our familia.

"First things first, tonight I collect Raina. I'll bring her back here," I tell my brothers. "Then we'll have a man on her when she's at school."

"You know, Franco, since we're not sure who is responsible, I can tail her." Matteo smirks, and I know exactly what he means. My brother is a player. He loves women. One, ten, fifty, it doesn't matter how many at a time, and it doesn't matter if they're married or not. As much as I trust him to do his job, she's my responsibility.

"You need to be at the warehouse," I inform him. He nods in understanding. "And you,"—I glance at Gio, who's still basking in the sunlight—"I want focused on Andrea. You're both going to take two soldiers with you at all times."

"Yes, Franco," Matteo responds.

For years, my father ran a tight ship. He did nothing by half measure. Only one hundred percent. Or nothing at all. What got him killed was the fact that he allowed himself to lower his guard against someone he considered a friend. Me, however, I don't have friends. That's why I will not go down like he did.

I should've been at the meeting last night. Lucio should've called me. But he probably didn't realize the danger he was in until it was too late.

"Let's get this done. I want to focus on going home soon."

They move without responding.

I will set my plan in motion soon enough, and I'll have a Mafia Princess by my side.

6

RAINA

The morning sunlight wakes me from a restless dream of a handsome man in an immaculate suit. Last night was strange. The way he looked at me was as if he knew me. But I don't know his name. He never offered it. The only thing that struck me was how much he reminded me of Lucio.

My heart aches again when I pick up my phone and open the message from Lucio's number. It makes little sense. *Why would he send this or even say this?*

I'm more confused by the time I get up. When I pad into the kitchen, I don't notice the package on the table. It's only when I settle in with my coffee that I see it. A silver box. Square, large enough to carry a necklace perhaps, but deep enough to hold something far more dangerous. Tied with a black ribbon, it beckons.

Tugging at the silk material, I allow it to fall free, then lift the lid. On the velvet cushion below is a gun. Silver glints in the morning light. The handle has hand carved wood where my fingers and palm would hold on to it. A small heart sits on the panel, and beneath it four letters two above the heart, and two below.

L. R. and R. L.

Lucio's and my initials.

My heart kicks in my chest painfully when I think about him. Lifting the weapon, I notice a small card attached. It's bound to the barrel with a string. I tug it free, setting the gun down, then read his scrawl.

BELLA, THERE'S NEVER A MOMENT I'M NOT WITH YOU. BUT WHEN I'm gone, you need to live too. Lucio x

SHAKING MY HEAD, I CLOSE MY EYES AND WILL THOSE WORDS away. I'm not sure where he is or why he has sent this to me, but something is amiss. My fear that he would be injured on one of his jobs has always made me anxious, and this right here only makes me wonder where the hell he is.

I'm not sure who would have left this in here, but I know Lucio always had his men watching me. They weren't obvious about it, but there were times their gazes would burn through me. If he's dead, one of them must have broken in, left this here, and it would have been under orders.

I know that nobody can have tomorrow guaranteed, especially in this life, but I never expected it would take Lucio from me. Whatever happened, I have a bad feeling about his disappearance. First my father, now the man I love. My chest is tight. My lungs struggle to pull in much-needed air. Even as I try to fight the wave of emotion, it holds me tight when I consider being alone in this world. I always thought Lucio would be around. I wanted him to be immortal, never leaving me. But I know it's not possible. It never was.

Thinking about both of them gone, murdered, it cuts. It

slices through me like a knife and I struggle to pull in air. My phone buzzes wildly on the table, distracting me from the pained thoughts of losing two men who meant the world to me. When I glance down, it's Lucio's number flashing on the screen. Swallowing the emotion that's choking me, I swipe my finger over the screen.

"Hello?"

"Ah, *Principessa*," a voice I don't recognize comes from the other side. A deep, foreboding tone that tells me he's not friendly. He's not family. And he's not calling to inform me that Lucio is alive.

"What do you want?"

"Sassy." He chuckles darkly. "Your boyfriend took from me, and I will soon take from him." The warning is clear. It sends an icy shiver down my spine, turning my posture rigid. "There will be consequences to his actions. And you, my dear, will ensure that his life was not a waste."

Was. Tears prick my eyes, and I will them not to fall. "Who are you?"

It's certainly not the man from the bar last night. His accent was far too distinct. The man I'm talking to now sounds older—with a deeper, gruffer voice.

"Who I am doesn't matter," he responds with another rumble of laughter that sets me on edge. "I will collect soon. And nobody can stop me." The line dies. I'm met with silence.

The gun that sits silently on the dark velvet is my only hope. To become like Lucio. To fight, kill, and maim. For years, I begged him to take me away. For us to run far away. But he always told me *soon.* Never a promise, just a word. *Did he know he was going to die?*

The loneliness I tampered earlier surfaces like a monster clawing its way through me. I'm alone. Andrea is nothing to me. He's merely a person I knew in another life. I haven't heard from my mother. I keep trying to call, but she's no longer answering. Anxiety tightens my stomach and I have a feeling that they have murdered her along with my father.

Perhaps she's beneath the water of the pier only minutes from the apartment. A wave of nausea hits like a wildfire, slamming into me, causing me to retch. Racing for the bathroom, I make it to the basin just in time. Nothing comes up because I haven't eaten in two days.

———

"You're late." Andrea's frustrated tone comes from behind me as I race into the office to drop my backpack. He stalks into the small space and settles behind the antique desk that was once where my father would sit when he came into the club. The thing is, my brother looks ever the asshole with his fingers pressed in a steeple, elbows on the desk.

"I had class. It ran over and I made it here as fast as I could."

"I agreed to your begging when you pleaded with me to allow you to go and study, but it shouldn't be interfering with business. I don't have a lot of staff on tonight, and for you to be late is unacceptable," he bites out.

Frustration and anger fuel me as I step toward the desk. "Do not speak to me like that. I'd like you to remember, I do this because Dad wanted me here, not for you. I'm here because it's my duty. If you have a problem with me study-ing, then fire me because I'm not giving that up." I shouldn't poke a sleeping bear, but he's really gotten under my skin tonight. Once I've finished my tirade, he rises. Leaning on the desk with flat palms, he gets in my face with a sinister smirk playing on his lips.

"Don't forget, little sister, I'm the one who holds the key to your trust fund. I can cut you off at any time with one click of a button, then you'll have nothing. Abso-fucking-lutley nothing. Do not fuck with me," he growls, sending fear racing through me.

Because he's the older sibling, he was granted the rights to our trust funds. Even though I'm over eighteen, my father's last will and testament stipulated Andrea as the head of the family, which gives him the right to pay us the whole amount or a monthly 'salary'. Of course, my brother being the asshole he is, decided to hold us hostage with our own money.

"I better get to work, since I'm late standing here arguing with you over something I have no control over." With that, I head into the bar and step behind the counter and take a quick glance around, noting there are two waitresses on staff tonight, both delivering a round of drinks. It's quiet now, but give it an hour and the place will be filled to the brim with immaculate suits, foul-smelling cigars, and the mixed scent of various expensive colognes.

"Hello, Raina." One of our waitresses, Shanique, places her tray on the counter as she greets me with a smile. She's a stunning girl with mocha skin and big brown eyes. I know my brother only hired her for her looks. He doesn't care what her goals are, and when I found them fucking over his desk, I knew she was only here for him. Not that it bothers me, but sometimes I wish he'd act like a brother instead of the heartless dickhead he's turned into since my father died.

"Hey, it's pretty quiet. Do you want to take your break now before the rush?"

"Sure, thanks." She nods with a grin, leaving her tray and stalking to the change rooms in the back.

Grabbing the tray, I place it behind the bar and start my

nightly routine of wiping down the counters and setting the glasses in rows, which will make them easier to pick up as it gets busier.

Only one thing can make this evening shift better and that's if a certain Italian stranger walks in, sweeps me off my feet, and rescues me from my hell. Kind of like Cinderella, slipping her foot in the glass slipper and leaving behind the evil stepmother and stepsisters. Only, I would never leave Adri behind.

Sighing, I continue my ritual to get ready, my mind still wandering to a certain dark-haired prince. I shouldn't think about him. He's dangerous, but I have a feeling he's nothing like Andrea. I doubt anyone can be as evil as he is. I've seen the terrible things he's done, and thankfully, I haven't been privy to it all. Deep down, I wanted nothing more than my freedom, and I wonder if he'll ever give it to me.

He enjoys the control. I cannot believe Dad gave him everything. Leaving my future in the hands of a bastard, he's inadvertently locked me in a prison I don't see myself escaping.

There has to be a way out.

I have to figure how to walk away from Andrea, from this life, and still have a future. Because if I stay, I doubt he'll allow me anything more than working in the club and obeying his every command.

7

FRANCO

My hand tightens around the thick neck of the man who looks like he's about to piss himself. My body shakes with rage as I regard him through narrowed eyes. A forty-five-year-old business owner who also deals in weapons. His front is a video store, which is laughable.

We provide services to anyone who needs it. Anyone who asks for it. But there's a price. Everything in life, everyone in life has a price. I'm about to take my pound of flesh, and I'm going to enjoy every damn moment of it.

Lifting the silver blade, I run the tip along his face, from his hairline down to the trembling lips of his mouth. Fear. It's an aphrodisiac to me. I'm a ruthless bastard. And mercy? It's unheard of when I walk in. "Look, I-I can p-pay when—"

"This right here," I murmur, venom dripping from my tone. Pressing the silver tip into his cheek until I see the tiny drop of crimson. Beautiful. Like a decadent Merlot. "This is why you should stick to your fucking agreements." I hiss in the asshole's face that's just lost all protection privileges by the Nostra.

"P-please I-I—" Gently, I push harder, interrupting his pleading. I watch as blood trickles down his cheek in an exquisite path over pale skin. "M-mo-money," he mumbles, pointing to the safe behind him.

"Gio, open the safe. What's the code?" I bite out, grinding my teeth as my jaw ticks in frustration.

"T-two, f-f-five, t-t-three, ei-eight, t-t-ten."

His whimpers are pissing me off. I want my fucking money and I want it now. "I don't play games, Mr. Jefferies. I don't like them at all," I warn, listening to the lock click and my brother tug the door open.

"All here." Gio smirks, taking the fifty grand and heading to the door. "Pleasure doing business with you, Mr. J."

I'm alone with the asshole, and there's no telling what I could do, but he did pay, so I'll show him how I deal with honest people.

Lifting my knee, I make contact with his crotch and the man goes down like a sack of fucking potatoes. Once again, I lift my leg, allowing my foot to slam against his jaw. The crack is audible and I smirk down at him in pleasure.

"I don't take lightly to games, Mr. Jefferies. Next time, I won't be so nice. Make no mistake." I lean in, my shoes pushing into his flattened hand. "I'm not a nice man at all." Then I step onto the knuckles perfectly until I hear the beautiful sound of broken bones. "As Gio said, pleasure doing business with you."

Slipping my blade into its sheath, I button up my jacket and head out the door with sex on my mind. Tonight, I'll need to find a gorgeous woman to fuck.

Hard, rough, and violent.

Preferably Raina Lombardi.

My mind isn't on work since it keeps wandering to what I'm about to offer Raina. I've never been this distracted over a woman before. There's something about her that's gripped me and I wonder if it's the innocence she exudes. She's a drug, a wicked sin that's burrowed into my veins, and I want to slide inside her over and over again.

My phone buzzes on the desktop. When I glance at the name on the screen, I can't help the anger bubbling up from my gut, racing through my veins.

"To what do I owe this pleasure, Cristiano?" My voice is ice, dripping with a poison I hope will kill the asshole wherever he is.

"Is that any way to greet me, *amico?*" We're not friends. Not anymore. Once I trusted this man with my life, but now... Now I'd prefer to see him lying in a pool of blood, gasping for his last breath.

"What do you want?"

A heavy sigh sounds through the speaker as he deliberates if he should play the asshole or just tell me what the fuck he wants.

"A meeting. Bring the contract and I'll look it over." He's been wanting in on our territory for years, since my father died. I've been pushing back because I don't trust him. I don't like him. In fact, I hate him, but he's got connections we need. Keep your friends close, but your enemies, if you don't kill them first, keep them even closer.

"And what makes you think I trust you enough to walk into your warehouse with your thugs guarding it?"

He chuckles then, a sound I remember from our younger years when we were close, when we were inseparable. He was like a brother to me. Then he fucked up. He took the life of a woman I loved. "If I wanted you dead, Moretti, you'd be six feet under by now."

I can't help laughing at that. "You're welcome to try, Russo, but I don't think you can handle killing me yourself."

"Two days, Franco. My warehouse on the pier in San Pedro. Bring your brothers. I'd love to see them again." Sarcasm is thick in his voice.

"Two days." I hang up before he can say any more.

Pushing up from my luxurious office chair, I head out of my office and into my wing of the mansion. In the bedroom, I pull my gym clothes from the closet and change from the three-piece suit into sweats and a T-shirt. Once I have my trainers on, I head into my personal gym. The treadmill always seems to clear my mind. Setting it to an uphill run, I set about attempting to forget about Cristiano, the man who almost fucked me over today, and focus on the pretty blonde.

I want her here. In my home so I can keep an eye on her. It's the least I can do since I was the cause of her losing her home. Only, she doesn't need to know what I did. My part in her father's demise will be kept a secret from the Lombardi princess.

Her father helped mine for many years, and I intend on repaying the favor by making sure she's safe from those who would still be out to hurt her. Perhaps this time I'll be the hero in her fairy tale. The knight in shining armor. Deep down, though, I know I'll never live up to that fantasy. She's too pure for me. I'll taint her with the darkness that follows me everywhere I go.

The sweat that trickles down my spine is at boiling point, not from the heat of my home gym, but from the temperature of my blood as I think about her. Picturing her on her knees. Seeing her smile when I touch her gently, yet firmly. After all the violence I've witnessed in my life and with all the blood on my hands, I wonder how I can even fathom my hands on her porcelain skin. I want her too much. I'll put her in danger by claiming she's mine. There are too many enemies out there wanting revenge and I'm their target.

As much as I don't want to admit it, I can't stop the desire I felt when I laid my eyes on her. Nothing is going to stop me, as wrong as it is. I'll have her.

She'll have to learn who I really am. I wonder if that would scare her away, or would it make her come closer until she's completely enveloped in the depravity of our family. The Nostra are dangerous men, with me as their leader. I wonder if she'd want to rule beside me.

Shaking my head, I try to clear the thought that's hit me like a sack of bricks. I'm getting ahead of myself now. Who knows if she'll want me near her.

Killing men who betray me makes me hard. I watch the life drain from their eyes and all I can think about is ramming inside a woman to see her eyes light with yearning. When I watch blood drip from a sleek blade, it makes me want to fuck a tight little cunt fast and deep. My lifestyle has opened my mind, given my body ways of reacting to what I do, and I find my release in sex. The stress of our jobs, of who we are, takes its toll and I've given in to the desire my body craves too many times to count.

My job comes with many obstacles. I run a business that doesn't allow for distractions. Many may see it differently, but being part of Cosa Nostra is something I've been born into. My family, originally from Sicily, on the southern tip of Italy, moved here to work alongside our American counterparts to take down the underground gangs trying to infiltrate the organization.

My father built a name for himself here, and since he was killed, I've taken over and I will not see the Moretti name go down. Even though there's nothing good about us, I can't see our family being dragged through the gutters.

When they told me to take over from my father, Franco Moretti Snr., I recalled the times I'd asked them to let me go. I wanted out when Dad died, but as the next in line, if I wanted to be released from my servitude, I'd have to be dead. Taking over what he started wasn't something I saw myself doing. Money laundering, loan sharking, drug trafficking.

Once I've secured the two new suppliers here, I'll make my way home, back to Italy. If I can lay low in Reggio Calabria for a few months after I've killed Cristiano, I'll be able to stay away from the shit storm it's going to bring about.

My first concern is my brothers. Gio and Matteo don't deserve this life. They should be out enjoying their youth, not carrying the latest Glock and slicing men to pieces because they didn't pay the protection fees. They shouldn't be worried about the new drug shipment coming in from Colombia.

"Franco." My brother's voice drags me from my morbid thoughts and I meet his dark glare. "I've spoken to the supplier, and they've confirmed the truck is arriving in the next day. Apparently, it's the coke those Brazilian fuckers promised. It's only two weeks late," he snorts in annoyance.

"Gio, I don't want you down there. I told you to send two men. I can't deal with you sitting in the warehouse with those two-faced pieces of shit. If they—"

"Relax, brother. I'm not going. I've decided to join you at The Gin Bar tonight. This girl has your head in a blender, and I'm intrigued to see how you handle her. Perhaps she has a friend." He chuckles. Pulling his cigarettes from his pocket, he regards me with a smirk when I glare at the damn cancer sticks he's holding. "*Calmati*, I'm going. Later, brother."

As soon as he leaves, I'm left sweating from the treadmill with my mind flitting back to Raina and what will happen tonight. I'd like to ruin her, only to polish her up again to ruin her repeatedly for my pleasure and hers. She'll find more pleasure with me than any other man she's ever been with.

With those blue eyes that remind me of a polished Moonstone, I want to see them tear up and glisten as she watches all the filthy things I am going to do to her.

La mia luna.

Shaking my head, I grab my hand towel and make my way back up to my bedroom. Our home is too big for three people, but with those two bringing home different women every night, I think it's safer that they're on the other end of the house.

My wing, on the west side of the mansion, encompasses my suite, bedroom and bathroom—as well as a living room and my personal movie theater. I enjoy my privacy and my brothers know that.

Stepping into my en suite, I turn on the shower and shove off my shorts and tug my T-shirt over my head, which is now laden with sweat. I pushed myself further today, hoping to clear my mind, but instead, I've formulated a plan. After tonight, she'll be mine.

I'll hire her. Giving her a job will allow her an insight to the type of man I can be. If she's scared off in the first week, I'll know I must move on. However, if the little temptress is still here after a week, I'll claim her. And that cunt of a brother who seems to think he owns her will have to live with it. Because if he tries to stop me, I'll provide him with a watery grave.

With my mind set on what I need to do, I step into the shower and allow the water to cascade down my taut muscles. Stress from the day washes away with the stream of hot water and I can't wait to have Raina in here with me.

To see her womanly curves as they drip with warm, soapy water, to feel the slickness of her cunt when I finger her against the tiled wall.

Glancing down, I find my cock jutting out, rock-solid, needing to feel a tight pussy pulsing around it. Fuck, I need to get her here as soon as possible. I grip my steel shaft and stroke it, imagining her mouth, lips, tongue, and fingers teasing me. To watch her swallow my cock down her delicate throat, choking and gagging on the length as I own her face, fucking it into submission with the rest of her body.

It doesn't take long for my release to shudder through me, sending me over the edge. Jet after jet of hot seed gets washed away and I ease myself back down to earth.

"Gio, are you ready?" Stalking into the ground floor living room, I find him at the bar. He's nursing a beer, which he immediately picks up and drains when he sees me. Pushing off the stool, he turns and shrugs on his leather jacket.

"Let's do this, old man." He chuckles beside me.

"*Vaffanculo*," I bite back, cursing him, but all I get is a chuckle from my little brother. He's twenty-nine. I'm thirty-eight. There are nine years between us, but he likes to remind me I'm getting old.

"I'll definitely be getting a fuck tonight, and it will be with a pretty pussy. That I can assure you of, Franco." Confidence oozes from him as we head to the SUV. Lorenzo has the engine running and once we're both seated, he heads down the long, winding driveway toward the large wrought-iron gates that keep us safe inside the property. Immediately thoughts of what I'm about to do invade my mind and suddenly, for the first time in a long while, I'm looking forward to seeing a woman.

I've killed men. Maimed them, cutting limbs from torsos without so much as a flinch, but knowing I'm about to meet those eyes that seemed to beg me to be her savior, I feel like a teenage boy who's about to go out on his first date. It makes no sense at all.

The ride is silent, which gives me time to gather my thoughts. I need to approach her with an offer she can't refuse, and if what I've learned about her trust fund is true, I know exactly how to reel her in. Her brother holds the bank accounts in his name, but I've got more money than God. I can offer her freedom if she chooses it. Only, in my line of work, freedom comes at a price. I wonder how much she's willing to pay.

When we pull up to The Gin Bar, I exit the car. Gio joins me as we make our way toward the entrance. The name above the door is lit up with green fluorescents. The doors are black with an awning held up by two silver poles. Two large bouncers dressed in all black man the entrance. When they notice our approach, both step aside and push the doors open as we near it. Recognition flits in their expressions and I'm sure they must have a mental list of everyone who's walked through the doors. I was here just yesterday, and I'm sure they remember. "Gentlemen," I offer a smirk. They nod silently as we pass.

Upon entering the decadent room that is furnished in black, silver, and charcoal colors, I make a beeline for the bar. I'm struck breathless when she smiles at a patron as she serves his drink. It's an easy, natural smile that seems to light her innocence from within and bathe her in an ethereal glow. Fuck, I need to have her light shine in me, under me, over me. "Not bad, not bad at all, Franco," my brother murmurs, and I know he's doing it to get under my skin.

"Why don't you go find yourself someone to annoy, Gio."

"I'm headed right for her," he informs me with a smile. When I follow his gaze, I notice it's locked on a pretty blonde sitting in a booth with a dark-haired girl seated opposite. Both incredibly beautiful, but it's when I notice the blonde glancing behind the bar and offering a wave to Raina that I notice the familiarity between the two.

"Gesù Cristo." My murmur halts my brother in his tracks, his gaze landing on me, and his brows furrowing in confusion.

He bites out, "What?"

"They're family, or best friends. I can't have you fucking around with her." I gesture with my chin at the girl in the booth.

When Giovanni takes her in, flitting his gaze between the two girls, he nods. "This is going to be fun," he jokes. Before I have time to stop him, he's already on his way to the two beauties with a confident stride. Shaking my head, I turn to the bar and settle in a stool. She's busy with a customer, but as soon as she sets his glass on the counter, her gaze snaps to mine as if she felt my presence.

Time stops. The sounds around us fall silent as if we're the only people in the dimly lit bar. The air is thick with unspoken desire, heavy with unbound lust, and swarming with unbidden need. "Raina." My accent and the rasp in my tone send a sensual shiver over her and as she makes her way toward me.

When she smiles, I'm enamored. I'm smitten. I'm fucking feral. The beast within me rages for her. To consume her every thought, every emotion, and ultimately, every orgasm. Everything she feels will be mine and mine alone. No other man will compare. I won't be her first, but I'll make sure to be her last. The thought comes to be without question, and I wonder if this little blonde will be able to tame the darkness within me.

"It's a little bit unfair, you know." She lifts a crystal tumbler that sparkles like her eyes and turns to grab the whisky I ordered yesterday.

"What is so unfair, Raina?" I question as she sets my drink on the counter atop a black square coaster with an image of a pearl in the center.

"You know my name and I don't know yours," she quips, a playful lilt in her voice. Regarding her, I lift the Scotch to my lips and take a long sip before setting the glass down. Control is essential when scoping out a mark, as well as a woman I want. She needs to trust that I can restrain myself when needed, but also, she has to remember, the predator that lies just beneath the surface is one that is ready for the hunt.

"If I tell you my name, *mio caro*, that will be the end of the anonymity. And who doesn't like a bit of mystery?" My question is light, tipping my head to the side. I meet her inquisitive gaze. She watches me intently, like she's waiting for me to do something.

Settling back, I drag my gaze over her face, taking in every inch of her smooth skin, creamy, unmarked. Her makeup is minimal, but her lips shimmer beneath the lights when she moves. Her golden hair is loose and hangs in waves to the middle of her back.

Today, she's wearing a shimmery silver tank top that looks like it's a size too big. I'd like to see the curve of her tits, but I'm not that lucky.

"Mystery can be detrimental. Secrets are dangerous." Her voice is just above a whisper.

"What if I told you I'm a dangerous man, Raina?" I breathe the end of her name, which earns me a beautiful blush on her cheeks.

"What if I told you I wasn't scared?" she counters. The flirtatious smile she gives me has my cock responding. The way she lifts her chin makes her even more beautiful. The sass she offers is something I enjoy, the banter with a woman who's not only beautiful, but intelligent enough to challenge me.

I'm alight with need. I'm hard with desire. I know without a doubt this woman will be in my bed, begging for me to take her, soon. I need to get my control back in this situation. She needs to learn where she belongs. *On her knees serving me.*

"Beautiful girls should be afraid. They should run in the opposite direction from men like me. I'm not a good person, Raina. Or would you prefer if I called you Rai?"

She shakes her head, scrunching her nose at the nickname. The action, though childish, only heightens my lust for her. I want to violate her innocence in so many delicious ways.

"I'm not like most girls." She leans in, as if she's about to tell me a secret. Her scent is soft, reminding me of fresh flowers, perhaps even candy. Sweet and intoxicating. A deadly combination. "My preferences may differ from girls you've been with, Mr...." She smirks then. It's a sinful smile on her rather innocent face.

"You're quite the inquisitive little thing. Aren't you?" I murmur, allowing my breath to fan over her face. Lifting the glass, I lean in, allowing the crystal to touch my lips. Her gaze drops to my mouth like I planned, as she watches me sip the harsh amber alcohol. I swallow, but her stare doesn't waver. She's fucking perfect. My tongue darts out, licking the remains of the expensive liquor from my lips, and I see her mimic the action. *Good girl.* So responsive. Flawless in every way.

The burn of the whiskey is enough to drag me from the

buzz that seems to swirl around us. "*Bella*, can I get some drinks?" Giovanni saunters over, breaking the stare down between me and Raina, which causes her to jolt to attention.

"Yes, of course. What can I get you?"

"A bottle of bubbly, Cristal please. Three glasses and whatever my brother is drinking." He slaps me on the back and chuckles. Her gaze darts between us, and I see her mind whirling with questions. Before she has time to say anything more, he glances at her and smiles. "Tonight please, beauty." His order angers me, but she obeys so easily, I can't help feeling proud of how beautifully submissive her nature is. "She'll be perfect, Franco," my brother murmurs and I nod in agreement. Yes, she will be. Both my brothers know my affliction, my need for a woman like this. But they also recognize how dangerous it is. How addictive it is.

As much as I should walk away, I don't. I won't. I'll have what I came for—the delicate blond beauty behind the bar.

8

RAINA

Both sets of eyes are burning a hole through me. I've never been devoured by a simple stare, but both these men are masters at it. It's almost as if they've undressed me and I'm at their mercy. The thought sends a heated tingle down my spine straight to my core and as I clench my thighs, the wetness pooling in my panties is an obvious sign they've affected me.

Men haven't given me so much attention. I've never wanted it, but with this stranger, I do. He hasn't told me his name and as much as I want to know, he's right. Perhaps it's the mystery of him that makes me so dizzy with need for him. Maybe if I knew who he was, I'd run a mile. *But what if I don't?*

Turning, I place the drinks on the counter and watch as the younger man places his credit card in front of me. "Leave that behind the bar. I think this evening will be a late one." He winks and leaves me alone with this hunter who's slowly turning me to a mess of desire.

When he settles himself beside my cousin, I can't help wondering what she's doing, since she's practically sitting in his lap. We don't know who they are, and from their private meeting with my brother, they can't be good people. "Does my brother intrigue you, Ms. Lombardi?" The seductive rumble from behind me startles me.

"No, he's just... I mean... that's my cousin and best friend."

"I know," he says quietly.

Snapping my gaze to his, I question, "What?"

"I'm guessing the dark-haired one must be your best friend. The little blonde my brother is so enamored with looks like you, so I'm going to hazard a guess that she's family of yours. The only difference I can see between the two of you is your eye color," he states matter-of-factly like I should have known he'd deduced our connection so easily.

"And your brother..."

"He's a good boy, perhaps annoying with his smoking, but he's not going to hurt her... unless she implicitly asks." He lifts his gaze to me in challenge, but this time I don't give him one. Dropping my eyes to the glass in front of him, I'm hypnotized by the way his index finger swirls the amber liquid. Once it's wet with whisky, he brings it up, pointing at me. "Taste it," he orders in a low rumble. It's gravelly, but the command is clear. Without a second thought, I lean in and wrap my lips around the tip of his finger. His mocha eyes darken further, turning black with desire.

This man is controlled, reserved, but the unbridled lust swimming in his dark eyes shows a beast lurking below his calm veneer. It's waiting to be unleashed, and God help me, but I want him to let loose on me. The deep-seated desire that emanates from him is enough to have my panties— which are still wet from earlier—drenched.

Once I've licked the alcohol from his finger, my mouth pops off with a soft sound. My gaze is locked on his as he in turn puts the digit in his mouth, licking the exact same spot

I did. I don't know why that's so sexy, but I've never been more turned on than I am now.

"Do you take orders easily, Raina?" Once again, he caresses my name the same way as his hands would stroke my skin. At least, how I imagine they would.

"Depends who's giving them." My sassy remark earns me a sexy smirk. One dark brow lifts in question and I shrug. "I don't know you—"

"You've just obeyed me when I told you to lick the alcohol from my finger, and from what I can see, you enjoyed it." The corner of his mouth lifts. It's the slightest movement, barely there, but I notice it. As with most of the things this man does, it's controlled.

"Maybe I was being polite so you'd tell me your name."

"You're really adamant. I like a woman with fire in her eyes." He lifts his tumbler and takes a long sip. His Adam's apple bobs as he swallows and the muscles in his neck are corded, as if he's barely holding onto the predator within.

"Since you like my fire, are you willing to give me something in return for it?"

"Franco," he says simply. My deductions on the accent were correct. He's Italian. Jesus, he's probably working for the American Nostra.

"You said earlier you're a bad man. Does that mean you're from the American organization or the Sicilian?" Tipping my head to the side, I regard him with sheer curiosity. Perhaps I've said too much, but I can't take it back now.

Dark eyes pierce me as if he's wielding a blade. "You know too much, little one." He smirks then, draining his glass. "Pour me one more and I'll give you one more fact, but you need to do something for me," he affirms with a nod, setting the glass on the counter.

"Okay. What do you want me to do?" He lifts his index finger, the one my tongue was swirling around moments ago, crooking it, ordering me closer with one small movement. Once again, I obey easily. Leaning in, I can feel the heat of his breath on my cheek.

"Do not make a scene. Go to the restroom, take your pretty pink panties off, and bring them to me. Then you'll pour me that drink. Now." His words, although not filthy, make me blush. He's asking me to do something so far outside my comfort zone. And when Adria's earlier comment hits me—*perhaps he's into those things you read about in those smutty books*—it makes sense.

Without responding, I straighten to full height and make my way to the back where our staff ladies' room is located. Locking the door behind me, I slip my panties off and bundle them in my hand. They're not pink, so he was wrong about one thing.

When I reach the bar, Franco is sitting alongside another man. An older gentleman with dark hair, which has a dusting of salt and pepper on the sides. Nearing them, the new stranger halts his words and regards me.

"Here she is. This is Raina." Franco smirks, glancing at my fist, and I know he can see the soft black material peeking out. "Please get Mr. De Luca a drink. He'll have the same as me," he says, reaching out his hand, palm up. "I'll take those." Shock races through me that he expects me to place my panties in his hand in front of the older man, who for some reason doesn't seem perturbed at the request.

"I... What—"

"Now."

One word.

A command.

An order.

I obey.

Placing the lace material in his hand, I feel my cheeks burning from embarrassment. He bunches a fist around it and places it in his pocket without so much as a glance at the older man.

"Good girl," he murmurs, then gestures to the bar. "The drinks now."

Without response, I turn to the counter and grab two tumblers. The bar is warm, but the fact that I have no panties on sends a shiver through me. Anticipation. The two men continue their conversation in Italian, so I can't understand what they're saying. I pour two generous measures of whisky in each glass. When I turn back to them, both sets of eyes are on me.

"Thank you, Raina." The older gentleman smiles, his ice blue eyes twinkling. The tone of his voice and accent match Franco's and I wonder if they're related, or if they're from the same organization.

"It's a pleasure. Let me know if you need anything more."

With that, I leave them to their business and continue serving the other patrons, getting drinks ready for my waitresses on shift. But I can't stop my gaze from flitting back to him. To Franco. He still owes me another fact about him, and I vow that before he leaves tonight, he'll give it to me.

As I serve drinks to customers, the thought of a man with my wet panties in his pocket sends a thrill through me. I wonder what he'll do with them. *Do I want to know?* Perhaps not.

An hour later, he rises, shakes hands with his friend, and the older man leaves. When he turns to me, he summons me with the crook of his finger. "I'm leaving, but I wanted to talk to you about something. In private." The last two words are uttered in a deep growl and I can't help squeezing my thighs together.

My vision's been stolen.

My senses are acute to the sound of soft footfalls.

Even though I can't see him, I know he's in the room. Even though the blindfold hides everything, my body prickles with awareness. The stranger with the rough, husky voice.

I know his name, but I don't use it.

I call him Sir.

I've seen his face. It's handsome, rugged even. Dark, piercing eyes, almost black, regard me with such intensity he steals my breath with a mere glance. His stare makes me feel like he's about to devour me. And he always does.

The gentle swish in the air has my ears thrumming with the sound. It's the swift sound of leather as it makes its way to my flesh.

The sting. The bite. The mark.

His breathing is even, controlled as he watches the tremble of my body. My back arches and my whimpers echo around us. When he first walked in, he ordered me to be quiet, so I bite my lip to keep from crying out. Another swish and my skin tingles and burns. The heat coursing through my veins and the thud of my heart against my ribcage send my mind into the abyss of pleasure.

Again, another lick of pain, hinting at the release that's coiling deep in my belly. The ache, the delicious need inside to find euphoria. I can no longer be still, and the gentle plea that falls from my lips is brash in the stillness of the room.

He doesn't move for a long while. I can feel him shift. The heat of his body is against mine with a swift movement. His lips whisper against my ear, "I'm going to take you now. I'll fuck your tight cunt. It won't be gentle or loving. It won't make you moan and plead yes. It will make tears fall from your eyes. You'll hate every minute I'm inside you. But you'll crave it every day. I'm going to make you scream, and when I'm done, you'll hurt. Collared. Bound. Mine. All mine."

JOLTING UP RIGHT, MY EYES SNAP OPEN AND I GLANCE AROUND, realizing I'm in my bedroom and not kneeling for the man who's been taunting my every waking thought. I think back to two nights ago with a small smile on my lips.

When Franco requested to speak to me, I led him over to one of the booths and we settled in the plush black suede seats. It's then that he offered me something I knew I couldn't refuse. He told me curtly what he wanted and expected of me. He also picked my brain, like he could read my every thought.

I explained about how unhappy I am working for Andrea and the future I want for myself, and in those few short moments, I wanted everything he had to offer. I was hooked. I didn't ask him to give my panties back. I didn't even question what he was going to do with them, but the thought made me smile. Then he left me with an envelope, sleek and stylish with the letter M in a swirled script. He ordered me to open it when I was alone in my room, which I obeyed.

When I got home that night, I made my way to my bedroom without so much as a glance around and ripped open the note. One page. Five simple rules. And the amount he's willing to pay.

LIKE ANYTHING ELSE, THIS IS A JOB OFFER. I'M OFFERING YOU A position as my personal assistant. There will be a formal contract for you to sign with terms and conditions. This is only an invita-

tion to accept the job offer set out for you. As my personal assistant, you'll work solely for me and my family.

You will not receive a salary. You'll receive a lump sum for your time. It is a six-month contract, which once it's run its course, you'll leave the mansion with your belongings as well as a healthy bank account.

It is important you know what you're getting into. Should you have any questions, you're welcome to send them to me. Alternatively, you'll send me a text message to the number at the bottom of this card to confirm you accept. You have forty-eight hours to think this through. Any later than that, the offer is moot.

The job is yours. Freedom is yours. The question is—how much are you willing to pay?

There are rules you will need to obey. There will be a non-disclosure agreement to sign. My family is connected throughout this country, as well as our home in Italy. You won't be in any danger, but you need to understand that there is always danger surrounding us.

Firstly, you'll move out of your home you're currently residing in and you will be given a suite in the mansion where you will live for the duration of your contract. This is non-negotiable. Obey my rules, and you'll find freedom.

RULE 1. OBEY EVERY ORDER. NO DEVIATING.

Rule 2. Do not question me. Ever.

Rule 3. There will be punishments, harsh ones.

Rule 4. Once you sign, you'll be property of the Morettis.

Rule 5. Relinquish all control over to me. I will own you.

$1, 000, 000 WILL BE TRANSFERRED TO YOUR BANK ACCOUNT. IF I receive your message and you agree, you'll get a text message

from me with your first instruction. Disobey and this ends here and you'll never see me again.

LAST NIGHT, I SENT HIM A MESSAGE AS INSTRUCTED FOR MY acceptance of his contract. Hence my email to my brother this morning with my resignation attached. It might be stupid to do this, but something about this man, his offer, and everything he's capable of draws me in. He's a hunter and I'm the prey caught in his feral jaws.

As I sip my coffee, I wonder what will happen once Andrea reads my email. There'll be hell to pay, but to be free of him is something I've prayed for. To have security, but to be able to continue my studies, is a dream come true. Franco is offering that to me. And I want it. I want him.

"Hey, chickadee." Spinning around, I find my best friend with her sweet smile watching me intently. "Care to tell me about the mystery man you've been daydreaming about these past few days? Is it the one from the bar undressing you with his eyes two nights ago?" she quips, her hip resting on the kitchen counter as she sips her coffee.

"In all honesty, there's nothing to tell, yet. All he did was offer me a job." I shrug, hoping she'll drop it because I don't want to talk about it. Not that there's much to say because I don't know what exactly is in store for me.

"A job, wow," she murmurs, watching me with dark eyes. "Come on, I know you're hiding shit." She pouts and I can't help giggling. There's no way I can tell her what he made me do. Or that he still has a pair of my sexiest panties in his possession.

"It's my first day, and at this stage I have no idea what to expect. He gave me an idea of what I'll be doing, but he also said I will need to live on the property." I gulp the last of my coffee and place the mug in the sink.

"Why would you need to live there?" Her question is something I've been wondering for two days. The longest forty-eight hours of my life. Hopefully, I'll have my answers soon enough.

"Once I know, you'll know," I remark with a shrug.

"Fine. But since your cousin is head over heels for Giovanni, I think I need to meet the other brother. Apparently Gio has a twin, and I'm so ready to see how Italians do it." She sighs dramatically. "Just make sure you give me all the dirty deets."

"I'll tell you if I meet the other brother." Shaking my head, I head into my bedroom before she can give me more of the third degree. I'm pulling my hair into a clip when my phone buzzes on the nightstand with the soft melody of a pop song I'm addicted to. Swiping my thumb over the screen, the message opens immediately.

No panties. No bra. Leave your hair down. The car is outside.

A shiver of excitement races down my spine. With a mischievous smile, I lift my skirt and shove the white panties down my thighs, tossing them into the laundry basket. Quickly unhooking my bra from underneath my top, I manage to pull the straps through the sleeves and out from the bottom of my shirt. My nipples harden at the cool air and my pussy tingles from being bare.

Grabbing my purse, keys, and phone, I race out the door, shouting a goodbye to Adria as I shut the apartment and run down the two flights of stairs. As he said, there's a sleek black Aston Martin sitting in the parking lot. The windows are dark and I can't see inside. Before I have time to really take it in, the older man who I recognize from the bar when he joined Franco for a drink gets out and rounds the rear of the vehicle.

"Hello, Mr. DeLuca," I greet with a shy smile.

"Good morning, Miss Lombardi." He offers a grin and opens the back door, allowing me to slip into the back seat. When I do, I find it empty. Without another word, I'm shut inside and moments later, making my way to the first day of work for the Morettis.

I have no way to know what it will entail, but the flurry of hummingbirds in my stomach tells me I'm in for something I've been craving my whole life. As the car weaves through the Los Angeles traffic, my mind recalls the last time I saw Franco and he offered me a job.

"I WANTED TO SPEAK TO YOU ALONE BECAUSE WHEN I DO ALL MY business deals, they're in privacy." The deep rumble of his tone makes me tingle in all the right places. When I glance up to meet his gaze, I'm knocked speechless. I realize I'm staring when he tips his head to the side. "Something wrong?" His question has me shaking my head. Then his gaze drops to my lips. "Raina." Even though I've looked at him a few times tonight, being this close to him, in a private booth, seems to have done something to my brain. Short-circuiting it to almost nothing.

Every nerve in my body feels as if it's been zapped with a live wire. "No, Sir," I breathe in a rush, watching as his gaze darkens and his lips lift into a smirk at my words. "I'm... I don't—"

He meets my gaze in a searing stare. Instead of answering, he lifts the crystal tumbler and brings it to his lips. How does this man make drinking whisky so sexy? Because God, I'm aching for an orgasm just watching his mouth and throat work the thick malt.

"Do you enjoy your job, Raina?" he asks, regarding me

intently.

"I'm... I guess. It's not what I want to do with my life, but it's my family obligation."

"And what are you studying?" He smiles, taking another drink of his whisky. Jesus, I think my ovaries may explode just watching this man. He's clearly older than me, distinguished and handsome. What could I offer him?

"How do you know I'm studying?"

He smirks at my question.

"I know everything about people I intend to employ, Raina. It's important to know who you're getting into bed with, as they say." His heated gaze pins me with a look that tells me there's much more promise in those words than he's letting on.

"Finance. Numbers are beautiful to me. My father gifted me his passion by allowing me to observe him. Not all the time, but there were special moments we could share the same love." My response is mumbled as I suddenly feel shy and silly with my frivolous topic. I glance down and swipe at the table, trying to keep my hands busy.

"Look at me."

Three words and my head snaps up. My blue eyes meet his dark ones.

"Family obligations are easy to remedy. Would you leave if you could?" The question has me frowning in confusion and he continues, "I'd like to hire you."

My body stills and I can't help staring at him, my mouth gaped.

"I... Do you even... I mean... Shit... Oh God, I'm sorry." Fumbling over my words, I cringe inwardly, hoping I haven't completely fucked this up. Franco comes from another world. I don't think I can even comprehend the things he does. Why would he want me to work for him? It doesn't make sense. "Do you have a bar? I mean... I don't—"

My words are halted by his index finger on my lips.

"Don't question me," he orders almost harshly. He slips an envelope across the table toward me. "Read this when you're alone tonight in your bedroom. It's my offer. Should you accept, the conditions, instructions, and rules are all there. If you have any questions, my number is on the card. I'm only a message away."

With that, he drains his glass and leaves me gaping at his broad, strong shoulders. He oozes control in such a sensual way, I'm in awe of his pull on me. The way his suit pants hug his thighs and ass have me ready to agree. To anything he wants.

HE'S STILL A MYSTERY TO ME. I DON'T KNOW MUCH ABOUT THE Morettis. I've heard them mentioned in the meetings my father used to have with clients, but I don't know what he does exactly. This is my chance at getting a new life, a fresh start from my father being murdered, to Lucio leaving.

A brand-new me.

Where I'm not the daughter of the man who'd been killed by his own clients. My father was responsible for his own death, leaving me and my cousin to fend for ourselves against Andrea.

I used to feel sadness. Now I feel anger.

The man who's offered me this job may be worse than my father, perhaps even a murderer, but I'm not scared. I've grown up around men like this. With their wealth and prolific estates that sit just outside the city, something of legends. My father spoke of them, told us stories to scare us, and I recall the intricacies of being part of Cosa Nostra. They live by a code of conduct. There's no doubt Franco is part of this dark familia. They're ruthless when it comes to killing and maiming. And as we weave through the traffic toward the outskirts of the city, I wonder what Franco has done to men who've crossed him. Perhaps even women.

I spent some time last night on Google, trying to read up on their ways, but I couldn't find much, so I was left wanting. All I recall from my childhood eavesdropping was how my father spoke of these elusive men. They dealt primarily in weapons and drugs. Anything you want, they can get.

There were many times I'd sneak into the room next to my father's office to listen to the conversations. My father didn't know I overheard him, but since then I've wondered about them. Intrigued by the mystery, even though I knew the secrets would be Daddy's downfall, I still found myself wanting more. Needing more.

Then later in life, before my father died, he had a meeting with one of his partners, Arturo, and they spoke about the Moretti mansion where who I'm guessing was Franco's father held lavish parties.

Where men dressed to kill, in more ways than one, and women, young enough, but legal, who kneeled at their feet, were a regular thing. Perhaps that's where my obsession came from. Wanting to know why women would do that.

Why kneel for a man?

I was just fifteen when I first met Lucio. He became my obsession. And deep down, I became his. As much as we were forbidden from ever going public with our relationship, I didn't want to stop seeing him. He never did anything more than kiss me back then. Even though I begged him for more, for his fingers to explore me, like I did to myself. But he stood strong on his convictions and waited until I was eighteen.

He was twenty-four the first time I laid my eyes on him, too old for me some would say, but for us, age didn't matter. It was how compatible we were mentally. I challenged him.

And then, when we finally had sex, our bodies fit

perfectly. So did our hearts. I fell. Hard and fast. Just like the way he used to fuck me.

He gave my body what it craved, my heart what it desired, and my mind what it imagined. There's no doubt Franco would offer me the same if I asked for it. But would he if he knew how pure I really am? I've only ever been with one man, Lucio. Perhaps he'll push me away, but I know how to play men like Franco Moretti, to taunt and tease them. That's why I find myself in a luxurious car that's taking me to something darker. More dangerous, but so deliciously sexy.

The car silently pulls up to two monstrous wrought-iron gates. As we wait, they glide open gracefully and the car eases up the long, windy, tree-lined driveway. The estate is immaculate. When the house comes into view, I can't stifle my gasp. It's incredible. Three floors of open brick with large white-framed windows. There are large potted plants on either side of the entrance with the most colorful, yet breathtaking hurricane lilies in them. The flower also known to grow in Hell. Perhaps I'm on my way there now.

The house exudes wealth. The second and third floors have terraces running from left to right with balcony doors, which I'm guessing are for each of the bedrooms. The ground floor has one bright red double door, which is the main entrance, paved with small cherry trees lining it. It oozes affluence without being superficial. The car comes to a stop and the driver exits to make his way to my door.

Once it opens and I step out, he offers me a bow and gestures with his hand to the door. "Mr. Moretti will be with you soon, miss." With that, I'm left alone, at the door to my future.

When I take in the door on closer inspection, I notice the gold knocker. The name Moretti lingers in my mind, and something clicks. Recognition. My heart that was beating wildly now leaps into my throat. It's him. It must be.

Before I have time to make sense of what I've just realized, the door opens. When I step inside, the spicy scent of his cologne envelops me and the smirk I've been picturing for two days straight beckons me.

"Welcome, Raina." He caresses my name with his tongue, lips, and voice as if he's making love to it. And everything south of my belly button tightens.

"Mr. Moretti, it's a pleasure." I offer a shy smile, although the thoughts of who he is threaten to steal my composure. The dark eyes that seem to pierce my soul narrow as he regards me quizzically. When I really look at him, I realize without a doubt, it's the young man from a photo I found long ago. But he's no longer as innocent-looking. He's a man.

"You've read the rules?" he questions, dragging me from lucid memories, and I nod. "Good. Let's get started." He doesn't wait for me to follow. He knows I will. He stalks toward the inner sanctum and I'm blown away by the modern lines, yet almost historic feel of the mansion. The artwork lining the walls has my eyes widening. All the Masters hang on the walls, from Van Gogh to Dali, from Picasso to Matisse.

The long hallway gives me time to collect myself, to calm my nerves, and to drink in the suited god of a man in front of me. The dark material molds to his form like it's been custom made for him. And I'm sure it has.

He oozes money, sex, and dominance.

Danger drips from his pores, but I don't find myself afraid.

Instead, I'm intrigued.

9

FRANCO

Leading her through my home, I find myself wanting to say something. To give her a tour of the beauty that lies within the walls, but I refrain for the moment. Her presence is distracting. The soft scent of her perfume wafts through the halls that once held parties so opulent, but hung heavy with depraved acts.

Most times, my father would host them. Other times, he would invite one of the suppliers to bring their clients or buyers here. I've seen things that have stayed with me.

She follows me two steps behind. I can feel her as if she were a storm about to rage through the house and destroy everything in its path. Even so, Raina is decadent, and I can't wait to see her break beneath me. Innocence radiates from her. I can see the blush on her cheeks when I regard her. Even though I know six months will never be enough with her, I realize I'll have to let her go once the contract is up.

I've put the wheels in motion, making sure that when she walks out the door, she'll have everything her father wanted for her. Once I've confirmed that her asshole brother no longer holds her freedom in his hands, she will no longer belong to me.

"Mr.—"

"I didn't ask you to speak," I grunt out. The need to spank her ass tingles over my palm. Reaching my office door, I push it open and step aside, allowing her to enter first. Jesus, if only I could see her in a thin silver collar. Her slim neck would look incredible with a small clasp hanging between her beautiful tits.

She's not slim. Instead, womanly curves have me hard as steel when I take in how the skirt she's wearing hugs her hips. The only thing that's currently running through my mind is to see her kneel before me while I make her eyes tear up.

However, at this stage, the first thing I need is for her to sign the contract and non-disclosure agreement. Once that's in place, she'll learn about her father, what her family means to mine. Most of all, she'll partner me to the upcoming ball.

I'll exact the revenge for her. In exchange, she'll give me what I want. Six months with her. In my house. In my bed. Nothing less. "I need you to sit, take a notepad from my desk, and I'll give you your orders. If you follow them—"

"I get rewarded?" Her interruption stirs the fuel in my blood. Stalking to my desk, I pick up the contract. It's thick and when I drop it on the wooden top, it thuds. Her gaze lands on it, then trails up to me. Meeting my gaze, she waits for me to respond.

"Let's get one thing clear, Ms. Lombardi. I'm your boss. When I'm speaking, do not interrupt me. When I give an order to speak, you're welcome to state your views. However, this doesn't mean I'll agree to them or adhere to them. Make no mistake, I'm an asshole, the biggest asshole you'll ever meet in your life. That is how I conduct all my business. Am I clear?"

She watches me in awe with those big doe eyes and all I can think of is watching her unravel. For her to let go of those restraints she's holding onto. Her poised stance, the straight back, and lifted chin show me her defiance. If only she knew what I did to little girls who want to play my game.

I await her retort. Instead, I'm pleasantly surprised when her response is a soft murmur. "Yes, sir." The creamy skin that turns a dick-hardening rosy hue has me biting back a groan. How I'd love to make her ass the same color as her cheeks. To have her bound bent over my desk as I punish her.

"Would you like to say something else?"

"I..." Her words taper off when she meets my stare. Her eyes glisten with unshed tears, causing my dick to jolt. It's so hard behind my slacks, I'm sure if I undo my suit jacket, she'll see exactly what I want to do to her.

"Well? I don't have all day, Ms. Lombardi. If you want to speak, then do so now."

"You, uhm, you told me not to wear anything under... I mean, underwear. I'm... I just thought you wanted—"

Stalking toward her, she halts her words and watches me.

Leaning in, my hands on the arms of the chair she's sitting in, I murmur, "Oh, I do want. This is part of your training, Raina. You see, I don't fuck girls who don't know how to hold themselves. You'll learn, and once you're ready, then I'll bend you over my desk, hike up your skirt, and see if that innocent little cunt can take my dick."

A gasp, sweet and gentle, falls from her lips and I'm tempted to train her mouth right now, but she's not ready. This needs time, coaxing. She needs to learn one day at a time, and I'm in no rush. I was going to talk to her about work, but I need to calm down.

"I'd like you to settle in at your desk. The computer is set up with your email and password. I have access to everything, so don't think you're going to come in here every day and chat with your friends. I'd like you to go through the appointments, make sure they're all synced to my calendar, type out the minutes of the meetings for the last two weeks, and get me coffee. Espresso. I'm sure you can handle it, can't you?"

She nods swiftly, and as soon as she rises, I catch a glimpse of pebbled nipples in her satin blouse.

Cazzo bella. Fucking beautiful.

"Yes, Mr. Moretti," she whispers, turns on her heel, and heads over to the desk I've set up in the corner of my office. Since I've got such a large space, I've decided to have her close, which will be easier to keep an eye on her.

"The kitchen is on the same floor. Walk out of the office, turn left, and head straight down the hallway. It's easy. Don't veer off. Do not enter any other rooms. If you need the restroom, I'll guide you." My order is gruff at best, coming off angry, but I'm far from it. She nods again and hastens out of my office. Immediately, it feels like I can finally breathe. This is going to be harder than I thought, and I'm not talking about my dick. "Franco! *Come stai?*" Giovanni saunters into the office like he owns the goddamn place.

"Brother, what the fuck are you doing here? You're meant to be overseeing—"

"Relax, it's taken care of. I have two of the men looking after both shipments, and besides, you told me you wanted me safe." He smirks, flopping into the chair opposite my desk, pulling a smoke from his black leather jacket, and flicking his Zippo while meeting my gaze. He knows I hate smoking in my office, but he always does it.

"I do, but you're meant to be on surveillance as a back-up," I hiss in anger, but I'm met with his relaxed expression, which frustrates me.

"Jesus, get laid, brother." He pushes up as the stunning blonde walks in with my coffee in hand. "Hello again, *bella*," he murmurs as she passes, setting my mug on the coaster.

Good girl.

Leaning back in my chair, I gesture to the beauty, introducing her to Gio. "This is my new assistant, Raina. She'll be dealing with the day-to-day schedule, so I'd like you on your best behavior," I inform him with a guarded tone. Our eyes meet and baby brother glares at me. My younger brothers, Gio and Matteo, may be approaching thirty, but it's at times like these, it feels as if they're still teenagers.

"I'm the handsome Moretti brother. It's good to finally meet you properly." He holds his hand out to Raina and she accepts with a small smile. She's shy around men and I wonder if it comes from an upbringing or if it's because of her past relationships. Although, I didn't see any links in the background check we've done on her, I doubt Matteo would miss anything.

"Nice to meet you, Gio." His name on her lips sounds like a song—melodic, gentle, yet fierce and erotic. *She's mine.* My brother knows how to taunt me. With his looks and flirtatious nature, he gets into the panties of women most men can only dream of. "You do realize smoking is bad for you," she quips, lifting her chin in defiance, and pride warms my chest.

"You sound just like my brother, mio caro," he murmurs the words *my dear* so low with their faces too close.

"Right, Gio. You have that meeting in an hour?"

A satisfied smirk lifts the corner of his mouth as he

quickly glances at me, knowing he's gotten under my skin. As he places a kiss on her knuckles my blood reaches boiling point. He's going to be sorry for taunting me with the woman I want.

"Of course, brother." He smiles, releasing Raina, and she immediately bustles to her desk. "Did you want those assholes to pay up today? I've spoken to Bianchi. He's begging for more time. I'm happy to slice some sense into him."

That's my brother. From flirting with a woman one minute to killing and slitting throats the next. Shaking my head, I think about how best to handle the asshole. He's been borrowing money for months without any payback. It's time we taught him the Moretti way.

Meeting Giovanni's eyes, I nod. "Do it."

With that, my brother stalks to the door, but before he leaves, he casts a gaze over at my pet. "See you soon, little one." Then he's gone.

"Your brother is a bit..."

Dragging my eyes to hers, I wait for her words, but she stalls.

"Tell me something, Raina."

Her gaze flits to mine as I unbutton my suit jacket and settle in my office chair.

"How did you feel last night when you realized I left the bar with your wet panties in my pocket?" The question earns me the exact response I wanted, a deep rosy color on her cheeks.

"I... Uhm..." The way she stumbles over her words is adorable. I want to train her how to be more confident, but still as submissive as she is now.

"Did you lie in bed last night imagining me stroking my cock with them? Perhaps inhaling your sweet, musky scent from them?" I quip and the color on her face deepens. To have that hue on her ass in the shape of my hand is so tempting.

"I didn't... I mean... You're so unfair." Pink lips pout as she regards me with that sassiness that's drawn me to her. So fucking innocent and tempting. I want to ruin her, break her, and put her pieces back together. To mend her in such a way that will leave her the perfect woman. The only problem is, I'll have to let her go once our six months are up, and I don't know if I'll be able to do it.

"Raina." Rising, I make my way toward her desk. Each step closer allows her scent to intensify, the sweet scent of flowers and candy. "Look at me. Meet my eyes and tell me if you're wet right now." Her lips part on a soft gasp and she nods. "Words. I need you to vocalize your needs, wants, and aches."

"Yes, sir. I'm wet."

"Good girl," I murmur and her body trembles in response. So fucking perfect. More so than any trained slave I've had. With that, I turn and leave her in the office. As soon as the door shuts, I smirk, heading toward Matteo's wing to talk to him about setting up a meeting when the new shipment of weapons arrives. It will give her time to calm down, and it will allow me a moment to get rid of this hard-on.

The office door is ajar when I reach it. Pushing it all the way open, I find my brother with a dark-haired girl on her knees before him. "Can you not close the door and lock it?"

The pretty girl gasps in shock, but my brother as always is unperturbed.

"Thank you, kitten. You can leave now," he murmurs, stroking her hair. She rises quickly on her four-inch heels and rushes through the door. Tucking himself back in his suit pants, he shrugs. "She was hungry. I had to do something about it."

"You mean you needed to get your dick sucked by... who was that?"

He doesn't meet my glare when he answers, "A girl I met two days ago. She's working at the warehouse counting."

"You're fucking our staff?" I hiss, but he shakes his head.

"Our supplier's staff."

"No wonder Zafretti is refusing to pay. He probably thinks you getting your dick wet is payment enough. This ends here. You want pussy, get it somewhere that doesn't involve our business." My anger fuels me. It always does. When I meet my brother's gaze, he nods.

"I fucked up. It won't happen again," he acknowledges, slipping into the expensive leather seat. "What did you need?"

"Set up a meeting with Russo. I want to get this deal done in six months. I want him behind bars where he belongs, or six feet under, preferably the latter. After that, I want to go home. Back to Sicily where this shit is far from our familia."

"You really want to go home?" He sounds surprised. When I was younger, I loved what we did. I enjoyed the hits we took out. I wanted to see the blood dripping from my hands. Now, I want more. I crave a normal life. Granted, there will always be the organization I run, but I don't want to be on the front line anymore. My time has come where I take a back seat and allow the younger members to take their place, earning their keep.

"Matteo, it's time I took on the role as mentor. This"—I wave my hand around his office, the weapons that adorn one wall have no allure for me anymore. The blades that my brother loves to wield so elegantly are no longer what I crave—"is not me. Not anymore."

"Are you going soft since you met the little blonde?" He chuckles, sitting back. He regards me with curiosity only my baby brother can muster.

"She is of no concern to you. Focus on your work. We need to make sure things run smoothly for the next six months. My personal life is mine."

"Fine. Just don't go falling in love with her, Franco. She's innocent. Our life isn't something you want to bring anyone into. It's dangerous. If they see she's your weakness, they'll fuck with it."

"Don't lecture me, Matteo. I know how to manage my personal life. Love isn't in my future. I'm going to enjoy her while I'm here. Once I get on that plane back to Europe, she'll walk away a millionaire and I'll enjoy my life on the beaches of Sicily. Now schedule that meeting. Let's get this show on the road."

With that, I turn and head out of his office with my little brother's warning on my mind. I've only ever felt or been in love once. She was special. Everything I ever wanted. My partner, my slave, and my fiancée. That is until my enemies found out and mutilated her so badly, I didn't recognize her body. They'd raped her, sliced her open, and left her to bleed on his white rug. I walked into the bedroom and rage fueled me. Hate wasn't something I'd allow myself to feel, but Cristiano Russo makes it an exception.

Now. Revenge will be mine.

So Matteo has nothing to concern himself about. My heart is firmly locked away. My cock, however, is hard and in need of a tight hole to fuck. Hence the little blonde who's going to spend six months in my office and dungeon.

IO

RAINA

Slipping off my shoes, I flop onto my bed and stare at the ceiling. The rest of the day went by without any more conversation between Franco and me. Mainly because he didn't return to his office. A message on my phone instructed me to finish up my first day early and the car would bring me home to sort out my things. Tomorrow when I go in to work, I'll be there for six months.

Needless to say, I was angry, disappointed. I wanted to see him again. To talk, flirt, perhaps to feel his mouth on mine. As much as I hate the way he spoke to me, something stirred inside me, which awakened a need for the violent delights he could offer.

When Gio walked back into the office, he didn't talk much, just explaining that Franco was indisposed for the rest of the afternoon. I wondered if that meant he was with another woman but shook my head to clear my mind of the frustration that brought.

He then handed me my contract and told me to read through it. Most of it is standard terms. I'm allowed to continue my studies, which was a concern I voiced to Franco the night he offered me the initial document. The rest is about my duties in the office, my hours, which surprisingly are flexible, and work with my college schedule. But it's the last ten pages that have my mind in a spin.

I'm going to be living with a man who wants me to be his slave. A sex slave. Someone who will be there for him to fuck, whip, and train. As much as that should scare me, it doesn't. My body hums with need.

Before I can replay everything that happened, my bedroom door flies open and there in all her glory is my cousin. "I want all the sexy details. Did you see Gio? What was it like?" Pushing up, I glance at her pretty brown eyes.

"It was... Strange. Yes, Giovanni was there, not for very long. I set up meetings, sent a few emails. It was like a normal office job, I guess." Shrugging, I wonder what lies ahead over the next six months.

"And Franco? What did he say to you?"

"Basically..." Sighing, I rise and pad over to my dresser. Grabbing a hair tie, I pull my waves into a messy bun and turn to her. "He wants me to be his assistant, but he also wants to fuck me. And he also wants me to move in. To live in the mansion for the duration of the contract. Six months."

"You're moving in with him?" she squeaks and I shake my head swiftly.

"Not *with* him, more like, in an apartment, or suite in the house."

She stares at me for a long while, and I know she wants to ask more than she has. It's written all over her face. I don't blame her. If we had swapped roles, I'd be forbidding her to go.

We've always been open about our lives and this is no different. I can't lie to her and tell her this is completely professional when it's far from it. The only thing I won't tell her is his strange kinkiness about taking my panties and possibly jerking off with them.

I also can't tell her about the emails I saw of what he did to the last man who stole from him. I stumbled upon the email to his brother by accident and needless to say, I'll have nightmares just from the description alone. I always knew the Cosa Nostra were violent, and looking at Franco, he oozes it, but to actually read about something he did with his own two hands, it changes my perspective.

"Are you scared of him?" As if she's reading my mind, her question drags me back to the present and I regard her earnestly.

"No." The answer is honest. I don't fear him. There's no inkling in his demeanor that tells me he'll hurt me, but others... That's another story.

I don't know what I'm getting myself into, or gotten myself into, but I know there's no turning back. I have to face the next six months of the contract head-on. I can't run. I can't hide. Not that I want to, but something tells me this man won't let me go easily.

The only problem is... Will my heart be able to let go when the time comes or will I fall? And if I do, I know it will be hard.

"Have you heard from Andrea? I emailed him my resignation, but he's been oddly quiet about it." The fear of what my brother will do when he gets his hands on me is enough for me to go willingly to Franco and hope he can protect me.

"He wasn't at work today. I know he was meant to be down in Miami for a few days. He said he was meeting a supplier, but..." her words taper off and I know there's something else going on with my brother. Something I'd rather not know about.

"I'm just... I mean, I've just left and you know what

Andrea is like." My tone is somber, and she nods. We all know what that asshole is capable of.

"Look, Franco will protect you, surely?"

I don't doubt it, so I nod in agreement.

"Then stop being such a sullen bitch and worrying about your brother. If he couldn't be bothered to call or respond to you, maybe he doesn't care. Come on, let's have a drink to celebrate your newfound freedom, and then I need to get ready for work. And my date with Giovanni." She giggles like an excited teenager.

"Tell me you're not going to fall for his brother. You do realize this isn't a game. They're dangerous, Cali." My warning tone sounds like something a mother would say, but I can't help worrying about my younger cousin. Even though she's only two years younger and an adult, sometimes, she can be irresponsible.

"No, we're having fun. I'm way too young to fall in love. Besides, you're the one who looks more forlorn than any of us. Also, tonight is a double date. Adria and Matteo are going to meet up and we're all going clubbing. Maybe you should come? Ask Franco to join us. Who knows, you might have some fun for a change."

I didn't want to go out, but my cousin can be frustrating when she's got an idea in her head and won't let it go. So, I find myself in the middle of a nightclub. The red and purple strobe lights swirl back and forth over the sweaty crowd and I'm watching my cousin and best friend dancing with the two brothers.

No, my courage to ask a man like Franco to come out to a nightclub is non-existent, hence me sitting here nursing a cocktail with a name I don't want to think about.

"Hey, a pretty girl like you shouldn't be sitting alone. Let's dance?" A drawl from beside me has my skin crawling. When I turn to find the source, I'm met with green eyes that almost seem luminous in the darkened club.

"No, thank you." I offer a smile and drag my gaze back over to the dance floor. My hopes that the stranger will go away are dashed when he slips into the seat beside me and grabs my wrist.

"You should be friendlier to people. It's rude to refuse a man a dance when he asked so politely," he hisses in my ear and fear snakes its way over my skin and collects in my chest. With my heart thudding wildly and the loud bass of the music, I can't find my voice to call for help. Neither Adria nor Calista are looking this way, and their dates are more entranced by the girls than casting an eye toward me.

"Please, just leave me alone," I plead, anxiety lacing my tone, and I fight to swallow the lump of panic that's silently trying to choke me.

"You're going to dance with me, pretty lady." The strength of his grip has my hand tingling from loss of blood, but before he can drag me off the seat, his hand falls away.

"Get your filthy hands off her. Now." A thick accent much like a rich chocolate fills the space and my head snaps around to find the dark eyes of Franco Moretti glaring at the man. "Either you take your vile hands off of her and find some other toy to play with, or I'll slice each finger from your limbs and have them stuffed down your throat." Each word is filled with a threat I have no doubt he can fulfill.

My gaze flits between my savior and my attacker. The drunken man leans in and hisses under his breath, "Russo says this isn't over, Moretti." And with that, he's gone.

"What are you doing here?" The question falls from my lips in a gasp as he circles one strong arm around my waist and tugs me against his solid form. Everything south of my belly button liquefies and my skin heats with the penetrating gaze he pins me with.

"Do you enjoy being sitting bait for assholes?"

His biting question sends me reeling and my feisty temper flares. "Obviously, you're here, aren't you?" As soon as the words are out of my mouth, I want to swallow them back in. With one strong hand holding me against him, the other comes up and fists my wavy locks, gripping my head tightly as he leans in. Our mouths only inches apart and the need for him to kiss me has me squeezing my thighs together to ease the ache.

"Do not piss me off, Raina. I don't take kindly to competition and men putting their hands on what's mine. That pretty little mouth of yours"—he halts for a moment, as if composing himself, dark eyes falling to my lips as my tongue darts out to moisten them—"will be fucked if you try to talk to me like that again. Do you understand me?" His grip on my hair tightens and a soft whimper falls from my lips. I should nod, I should agree, but the alcohol racing through my veins, coupled with the desire he stokes like a fire in my core, has my mouth working to my disadvantage.

"Don't make promises you don't intend to keep, sir," my murmur is like fuel, which sets him alight. His body visibly vibrates as he grips both my hips, lifting me and walking toward the rear of the VIP section where we've been seated. We come to a stop when my back hits the wall and he presses his body against mine.

"You want this, *bella*?" He calls me beautiful in Italian, which only intensifies my yearning. "Because, once I take you, once I fuck you, your body will no longer be the same. You'll hurt, sweetheart. You'll cry and beg and scream." He hisses so violently, but his words don't scare me, they caress me. They stroke my skin, they ignite my blood, and my panties are drenched.

"I want this."

That's all he needed. His one hand deftly finds the hem of my dress, lifting it to my hips. His fingers stroke the wetness between my thighs and he audibly groans when he finds the material damp.

"Jesus, Raina, you're fucking wet for me," he moans as his lips find my neck. They feather along the sensitive skin, causing goose bumps to rise in their wake. When he shifts my panties to the side, he slips a finger into my molten core. I'm slick, needy, and my fingers find purchase on his shoulders. "Spread your fucking legs for me," he grunts, pressing himself against my thigh. I can feel the thick, hard length of his erection.

"More, please," I beg. I plead. I whimper. Suddenly, two thick fingers delve into my pussy. In and out. Deeper. Faster. My legs tremble and my body arches toward him. I'm needy. I'm wet. I'm about to unravel for this man.

"I'm going to whip your ass so hard for making me do this, but fuck, I need to feel you come. Do it. Now. Soak my hand in your juices, Raina," he growls, his teeth sinking into the smooth skin of my neck as he sucks the flesh into his mouth. His digits crook inside me, pressing against the front wall of my pussy, and I explode.

My knees give out and if he wasn't pressed against me, I'd never be able to stand on my own. My eyes shut so tight all I see are white lights. My body pulses around his fingers and I know I've soaked his hand.

Moments, perhaps hours, later when my eyes flutter open, I find dark chocolate pools bearing down on me. "You're exquisite when you're lost in lust and desire, *bella*," he murmurs reverently. A smirk tugs at his lips and he steps back. Taking a look around, I realize we're still in the club. Nobody's even noticed us.

"How long—"

"Only a few minutes. You were so beautiful flying so high, so graceful." He reaches up with the hand that had given me the best orgasm of my life, and he smiles. "Taste yourself," he whispers and I do. Sucking both digits into my mouth, my essence both sweet and musky coats my tongue. Before I have a moment to think, he pulls them from my lips and crashes his mouth on mine. Unapologetically, his tongue sweeps into my mouth. It's violent, like the man himself. It's rough, sexy, and as I allow him to explore my mouth with his, he steals every breath, every sound, and I know he's about to steal my very soul.

When our mouths finally part, I'm breathless and so is he. "Franco," I breathe his name, but he places a finger on my lips, silencing me.

"Don't. The only thing I need to hear from you is you saying yes."

"Yes?" My brows crease in confusion as our eyes meld into each other. This man is danger with a capital D, but he's also a mystery. Tiny hidden pieces of one solid story that I'd like to uncover. Each moment I spend with him, something small is revealed to me. Whether it's the way he looks at me, something he says. My curiosity wins out, and I find myself wanting to know all the parts of the cryptic Franco Moretti.

"I want you, Raina. But, as much as I want you, I'm warning you, I'll hurt you. Physically, mentally, and emotionally. My life is... difficult. I can't give you forever, but for now, give me you. Offer yourself to me, *bella.* Let me have your body. Just promise me you will not fall in love. This"—he gestures between us—"isn't love. It can never be love. It's a contract. An agreement you've read. It's fucking. It's brutal, ruthless, and violent. If you can handle that, then I want you to say yes right here, right now."

"If I say yes, what happens? Do I just become your

what... slave? Submissive? Fuck toy? You use me when you need me and I'm pushed into a corner when you don't?" My words are angry, heated with frustration at his push and pull.

"Slave? Submissive? Fuck toy? I like your descriptors, little one. Perhaps all three. I mistook you for an innocent. Someone new to this life, but it seems you're not?" he questions and I can't help blushing.

"I read a lot," I retort, but his gaze narrows, as if he doesn't believe me. "So, what happens? Tell me here and now, or I'll walk away." I watch his eyes flash with something. Fear? I can't tell because he quickly hides behind a mask of cool control.

"No, you'll have your job, but at night, you'll be mine to use as I see fit." He takes a step back to regard me. With narrowed eyes, I watch his eyes flicker with emotion. As much as this man tells me he doesn't want love or won't welcome it, there's something in the way he looks at me that screams otherwise. "This is sex. It's a business agreement. My life is my work. My love is my familia. There's no room for more. If that's what you're looking for, then this ends here."

The thought of him walking away burns. It hits me deep in my gut, but I find myself nodding. "Okay." It's a soft, murmured word that echoes around us.

"Yes?"

"Yes."

II

FRANCO

When she said *yes*, something inside me shifted. It was an emotion I didn't need or want. So, as I gripped her hand and tugged her behind me, I shut it away. Even though the look on her face when I told her this would end if she didn't agree screamed at me to walk away, I couldn't. I held my fucking breath until she uttered the word *yes*. Then my world tipped on its axis.

Steeling my gaze, I stalk through the crowd with her body close to mine. My brothers are sitting in a booth with their women when I reach them. "We're leaving. Don't cause shit, but Russo's men are here. I want you to stay with these two." I point at the two girls on each of my brothers' arms.

Both nod. They understand the danger we're putting these girls in, but I refuse to allow an asshole to rule my life.

"Where are you going, brother?" Matteo smirks. He knows. He wants me to confess that I've got feelings for her—more than just claiming her—but I won't.

Shrugging, I tug her into my arms and pierce my brother with a warning glare. "I'll see you tomorrow."

That's all I say before I turn and walk away with Raina's hand in mine. When we reach the car, I open the door and allow her to slip into the seat. Once I've joined her, I signal for my driver to get us back to the mansion.

She's silent, with a nervous energy that whirls around her.

"Are you afraid, *bella*?" Her gaze lands on mine. The softness of her skin calls to me. Big eyes lock on mine and she squares her shoulders as if she's about to tell me something I won't like.

"No, I can't be scared of you, Franco." She purrs my name, which has my cock hardening behind the steel of my zipper. A smirk lifts my mouth as I watch her.

"And why is that, Raina?"

"Because I want you. Your darkness, your mark. Something about it calls to me. As if I was made for it…" Her words taper off into silence. I want to respond. To tell her how much I wish she were made for me, but I don't. Because this isn't anything more than a fuck. A contract between two consenting adults.

Once I use her the first time, there is no guarantee she'll come back. There isn't a surety that she will want what I have to offer. So I stay silent.

"Do you ever think about a different life?" Her question burns through the thick tension that radiates in the car as we weave closer to our destination. To the dungeon. The room I'm about to tie her up in and fuck her until she can't walk.

"No. I told you. My familia are my brothers, my *cosca*." With that, I turn and watch the tree-lined drive inch us to the house. Once the car stops, I exit and reach for her. Moments pass and I wonder if she's going to request to go home, but she doesn't. Instead, she slips her hand in mine and joins me on the gravel. Meeting Lorenzo's gaze, I give him a swift nod. "Thank you, I'll see you in the morning."

He's been my driver for eight years. He's seen things that would make any grown man shudder, but he's also had his family mauled by the assholes we're trying to take down, so his loyalty is with the Morettis and what we can do.

Turning, I tug my new pet toward the door. Inside, I lead her toward the east wing where my suite lies waiting. Every step closer, I wait for her to refuse. I expect her to tell me to stop and take her home. But with each clip of her heels, the tension that stifled me in the car dissipates and she comes to me willingly.

Once we've reached the doorway to the room I keep hidden, I unlock it with the small gold key and push it open. With a soft creak, it gapes, begging us to enter and enjoy the delights it has to offer. "After you, *mio caro*." Gesturing with my hand, I allow the beauty to enter.

In the silence of the room, she steps tentatively deeper into my world. My fortress of dark pleasures. When you've seen the heinous things I have, you need an escape from the consistent, everyday horrors.

This... This is my haven.

"I..." Her voice is raspy, and I wonder if it's from shock, fear, or desire. Perhaps all three. What an intoxicating feeling.

"Do you want to leave? We can go into the living room."

She shakes her head. Reaching out, she strokes the leather of my favorite whip. There's a reverence in her touch. Almost as if the thought of having it mark her has consumed her thoughts.

Her fingers brush over the wood of the cane that lies on the table. It's a featherlight touch and I can't stop the thoughts of having her hands on me in the same way. I'm about to say something when she toes off the heels she's wearing. Leaning down, she scoops them up and pads over to the small dresser where I keep my toys, everything from butt plugs to dildos and clamps. She sets them side by side on the floor and rises to full height, which without her heels is only a mere five-four.

Wordlessly, she unbuttons her blouse, pushing it off her shoulders as she taunts me unknowingly with a striptease that isn't meant to be erotic, but I find myself rock-hard. There's no inkling about her movements that shows if she realizes how beautiful, how powerful she is.

When she finally turns to me, she's dressed in only a pair of sheer blue panties and a bra to match. Her body is curvy, delicious, sexy. Everything about her has my mouth watering to devour her. To taste her sweetness on my tongue, my fingers, and feel her unravel while my cock is buried deep inside her cunt.

She drops to her knees, spreading her legs, with her eyes on the floor before her. My restraint snaps and I close the distance between us. As soon as I step into her line of vision, I crouch down and reach for her chin. Lifting her head so she's looking directly at me. "You know how to present yourself?"

"Yes, Sir," she murmurs, the words breathy, in a sensual tone. "I told you, I read a lot." A small, intimate smile passes her lips, then it's gone. Our eyes are locked for long moments.

"And you've never been owned before?"

She shakes her head.

Relief floods me and I nod. Stepping back, I rake my gaze over her body once more before I question, "You're sure you want this? You're not going to run away when I hurt you?"

"No, Sir."

Two words and I'm about to come in my slacks. It's been too long and the need that courses through my veins has me hungry. Ravenous. Starving for a taste.

"Stand. Go over to the bench, get those beautiful breasts out, bend at the waist, and spread your legs."

Without response, just a simple nod, she obeys my command. This woman has been born for this life. Her body exudes it.

Once she's in position, I unbutton my shirt, pulling it from the waistband of my pants, I shrug it off and allow it to pool behind me. My mind is a mess. Clarity is something of the past when I kneel behind her and inhale her womanly scent.

She's drenched from her earlier orgasm and from the position I've just put her in. Reaching up, I grip her ass and squeeze it hard. A soft whimper escapes her lips, and she pushes back against my hands. She needs this as much as I do. "You're beautiful, every inch of you, Raina," my murmur dots her skin with goose bumps and she shivers in my hold.

Leaning in, I run the tip of my nose from the back of her knee up the smooth skin of her thigh. When I reach her sex, I copy the motion on her other leg. The scent of her pussy drugs me. It runs through my veins and I need more. I want to taste her. Hooking my fingers into the waistband of her panties, I tug them from her hips and as they slip down to her knees, I'm awarded with a sight that stops my breath.

Her glistening lips beg me for attention. Pink. Wet. Mine. Once again, I grasp the cheeks of her ass and open her to my gaze. Flattening my tongue, I gently lick from her hooded clit to the forbidden entrance of her ass. Her taste lingers on my tongue, taunting me, knowing I can't deny how much I want her.

"Please." Her sigh is music to my ears, but she's spoken

out of turn. Raising my hand, I rain down a swat on her bare ass and a yelp falls from her lips.

"I didn't ask you to speak. Remember the rules, or you will be punished," I warn, my tone dripping with dominance. Once she's quiet, I lap at her core again, reveling in her sweetness. The slickness of her arousal that coats my tongue and I never want to rid myself of it.

Her body shivers and her knees buckle. Holding her up, I rise to full height, towering over her bent form. Having her here in this room with her body for me to use as I wish, her submission is more than intoxicating. It's got me aching to feel her cunt squeezing my cock.

"Stand, turn, and face me."

When her blue eyes meet mine, they glisten with desire. Hunger for more. I lean in, brushing my lips, which are wet with her arousal, on hers. Allowing her to taste, smell, and savor the sweetness.

"You like the taste of your pussy on my lips?" I question with an amused stare and she nods. "Words, *mio caro*."

"Yes, Sir. I love tasting what you do to me." She smirks. Sassy little brat. Gripping her hips, I spin her around and press a hand to the small of her back, which has her bending at the waist. Without warning, I rain a swat on her ass, so hard and fast it knocks a *whoosh* of breath from her.

I gift her another and another. Until her skin is red and marked with my hand. My hands stroke the skin, sending ripples through her body. Her knees are barely holding her up and I know what my next step is. She'll be bound while I test her limits. She'd look so beautiful with my cane marks on her ass. Pretty purple bruises telling her she's mine. Every time she sits, moves, walks, I want her to remember who she belongs to.

Me.

"Raina, stand. I want you to go over to the table in the

corner, near the window. I want you to kneel on the table facing outside."

Silently, she obeys every word to the T. No argument, no question.

I watch her, in awe of the beauty and perfection. Once she's kneeling, I step up behind her. With her on the small table, it puts us at the same height.

"Look across the field. There's nothing and nobody. You're here alone with me. Only me. Do you feel safe?"

She nods.

"Now, before we start, you need a safe word."

"I don't—"

"Trust me, *bella*, you'll need one."

Silence once again falls around us like a song. This is our song, our symphony, which echoes around us, playing to the movement of our chests as they rise and fall with every breath. Almost poetically. This is what I live for. The anticipation of what's to come.

"Whisky," she murmurs. A chuckle rumbles in my throat at her choice.

"Is there a reason you chose that word?"

She smiles shyly. The reflection of her face in the window makes me grin, something I've not done with a woman in a long while. There's a lot I want to do with Raina that makes me wonder what hold this woman has on me. "It reminds me of when I first saw you drinking the whisky I poured. The way your lips glistened with the alcohol, and I wanted to—"

"Lick it off?" I quip, finishing her sentence, and she nods. Running my fingers over her bare shoulders, I trail my touch over her breasts, missing her nipples that have hardened beautifully. When I reach her hips, she gasps lightly. "Ticklish?"

An affirmative nod.

"Tell me, *bella,* that night, did you go home and touch yourself?"

A gasp, erotically charged, blazes through her and into me. As if we're tethered to one another and any movement she makes, passes through me.

"Did you, Raina?"

12

RAINA

"Did you, Raina?" His question hangs in the air, teasing me.

"Yes, Sir." My answer is a raspy murmur. The heat of his body against my back has me leaning into him, needing the warmth.

"Did you think about how it would feel if my hands were stroking your skin?" As he voices the question, the tender and gentle way he's touching me has my body pulsing, needing him to fill me. We've kissed, he's had his fingers inside me and his lips on my pussy, but it feels as if we've been connected, melding to each other.

"Yes." My whisper is hoarse. A harsh slap on my left breast has me yelping loudly.

"Yes, what?"

"Yes, Sir."

A deep rumble stirs in his chest at my words. "Good girl, don't forget where we are. Not even for a moment. Remember, Raina, I'll hurt you because I want to. Because it pleases me. And because I'll come harder when your cheeks are tear-stained, when your bottom lip is trembling, and your smooth, creamy skin is red and glowing."

"I've thought about you since that first night. Every moment since, you've consumed my thoughts. You've gripped my mind," I murmur.

"I know, *bella*." He steps away from me then. The heat that cocooned me is gone and a shiver races down my spine. "Remember your safe word," he warns. A sound from behind me has my senses alert. I can't see him because I'm staring out the window, but I feel the shift of air in the room as he moves around. The swish of a whip hisses through the air. "Keep your eyes on the lights outside." That's all he says before the sting on my ass has me yelping.

Another bite comes and another. As much as I thought it would hurt, and fear would override my curiosity, it's not. I find myself growing wetter with each thwack against my sensitive skin. I await the eleventh one, but it doesn't come. Instead, his hands caress the now reddened and tingly flesh of my ass.

The view becomes blurry as the tears threaten my eyes. They pool on the edge of my lashes, but I don't blink. The twinkling lights below us shimmer as he manipulates my body. I've never felt such desire from a mere touch. Let alone achy and needy from being spanked, whipped. Whatever he did to me it feels as if he's lit a match and I'm slowly burning from the inside out. As if molten lava is slowly swirling deep in my core and he's the only one who can extinguish it.

"Is your cunt wet for me?"

"Yes, Sir." I nod, hoping with everything I am that he'll touch me where I need it. That his fingers will find my clit and tug it, tweak it till I'm whimpering. That he'll drive his cock so deep inside me I'll forget my own name just from screaming his.

It's quiet for a while, then I hear the crack of a bottle being opened, a glass being set on a surface, and the swish and swill of liquid being poured into it. Not long after, his order comes.

"Turn around, sit on the table, and spread your legs." His voice sounds far away, and when I turn, I find him seated in a leather armchair, his legs spread and his bare torso bathed in the soft moonlight shining through the window. Dark eyes pierce me. They bore into me inquisitively as if I'm a caged animal in the zoo and he's curious about me.

A slow, sensual trail ignites my skin as his eyes rake over me. Drinking in every inch of my bare body, he lifts his glass I didn't notice he was holding and takes a long sip of the amber liquid. With the heavy silence in the room, my heartbeat echoes in my ears.

After another minute of him watching me, he sits forward, elbows on his knees. The corner of his mouth lifts into a smirk so deadly, so filled with heat that I'm about to explode from just watching it curl his lips. "Touch your cunt." Three words send my mind reeling and I reach between my thighs. My sex is drenched, my fingers dip into my body, and my head falls back as pleasure sends electric tingles through me. Every inch of my body is alight. I'm an open flame and I wonder if he'll have the courage to get burned. He rises, closing the distance between us, and when he finally reaches me, he leans in. His mouth mere inches from mine and my tongue darts out to moisten my lips with the anticipation of a kiss. But he doesn't crash his mouth to mine. Instead, he murmurs, "When we're in here"—his gaze flits around the room—"you're my slut. I will refer to this"—his hand reaches for my pussy and he cups it, dipping one long digit into me, which joins my fingers—"as my cunt. I own you. Every hole. Every inch of your body. No other man will touch you. No other man will stick his dick in my possession. Do you understand me?"

His words, though filthy, almost degrading, have me on the brink of an orgasm so fierce, I doubt I'll be able to hold on for much longer, but I answer, "Yes, Sir."

"Your orgasm is mine. When you come, it will be with me or for me. Under my orders. Now"—he drags his finger from my lips—"take your glistening fingers and suck them clean."

I obey his order, lifting my hand to my mouth. I lick each digit, tasting my essence on them. The sweet, musky scent and flavor is something I've only ever tasted from him. My first time. And it seems not my last.

Yes, my past has been twisted, violent, and dark, and Franco seems to know that instinctively. He feeds the craving that courses through my veins. I watch as Franco licks my juices from his finger. But he doesn't just lick it clean, he savors it.

"I'm guessing you're needy. Your release is on the edge, isn't it, *mio caro*?"

I nod and he chuckles. Crooking his finger, he gestures toward the bed I'd seen earlier and I stand on shaky legs to follow him to the dark silk sheets. The blue reminds me of the midnight sky, and the four-poster bed is reminiscent to an antique bed you'd find in a castle.

"On the bed. Do you want to watch me fuck you? Or do you prefer being on your knees, Raina?"

My gaze snaps to his in surprise. I didn't think I'd have a choice.

"I'm an asshole, not a monster," he murmurs on a chuckle.

"It depends who you ask." My retort earns me a heated glare and I know I've fucked up royally. His one hand grips the hair at my nape and he drags me to the foot end of the bed.

His lips are on my ear as he hisses, "And just who would you ask?"

"I don't... I mean... I didn't..."

"You knew what I was. You agreed to come here. Do you like when I hurt you? Does it make your little cunt wet when I manhandle you? Tell me, Raina. Do you want me to release the beast that hides inside me to rip you apart? To fuck you raw until you can't walk?" Everything below my belly button tightens so painfully I whimper. A moan low in my chest rumbles with desire, with need so great I'm shocked speechless that this man, so violent and dangerous, has my body so needy that I want what he's offering.

I need the beast. I want the power. And I realize what it is as he bends me over, pressing my face to the cool silk sheets. It's something I've never had. Never experienced. Raw, animalistic passion.

"Yes, Sir. Give me your worst."

With that, the swish of material of his slacks finds the floor. I hear movement, but I can't see him. And with one relentless, violent drive, he's buried inside me so fucking deep my lungs forget how to work. My fingers fist the material below them, my knuckles turning white. And the release, that taunting bitch, she attacks me with such force, when he pulls out and thrusts back in, his hips bucking against me, our skin slapping loudly, and the vise grip he's got on my hips all send me over and I'm flying.

My eyes slam shut as he fucks me. This is not lovemaking. This is far from sex. This is brutal. The pain and pleasure that shoot through my veins have me crying out his name. Chanting it. Moaning it. And I realize he's attempting to fuck the memory of Lucio from my mind, from my body. But he's also fucking any man who may be with me in the future into oblivion.

"*Mio caro*, Raina," he murmurs as his body slams me

into the bed. He fists my hair, tugging me up against his chest. His lips on my neck as he repeats my name over and over again.

"Franco," I hiss through my teeth as his cock hits a spot inside me I've long forgotten. We're feral with this basal connection.

"Come with me, Raina. Coat my dick with the sweet juices of your cunt." And with that, he drives so deep it's as if he's trying to shatter my soul with his cock. As if we're molding ourselves into one person. And I explode. Stars burst behind my eyelids and I cry out, screeching out his name.

The jets of heat he fills me with send me spiraling into an abyss so beautiful I never want to leave.

A FEATHERLIGHT TOUCH STIRS ME FROM MY DREAMS. MY BONELESS body tingles and my eyes crack open to find deep brown pools gazing back at me. The smirk on lips that devoured not only my mouth, but most of my body as well, tilt in a playful way and I wonder what happened to the dominating force that fucked me into a sleepy stupor not that long ago.

"You're quite the vision when you're asleep, Raina," he murmurs almost reverently, which has my heart catapulting in my chest. He said we're only here because of the contract. Nothing more, but this, this definitely feels like more. Pushing up, I grip the sheet and cover my breasts, and he chuckles. "I've seen those, and so much more of you. Don't hide from me, baby."

"So... what is this?" I gesture between us because I've never learned how to keep my mouth shut, and this time, I'm sure it's going to land me into trouble.

"What do you mean?" The tone of his question is almost vacant of emotion. As if he's shut down and I know once he does, there's no dragging him back.

"Watching me while I sleep, telling me I'm a vision. That's all romantic shit. Things you don't do?" My question hangs in the air between us as I regard him with a questioning gaze. He lifts chocolate pools to my ocean-colored ones. I've never been good with compartmentalizing my feelings and I realize this will be my downfall in agreeing to his contract.

To his terms. After what we did, the intimacy of what I gave him, what we shared, it's somehow burrowed itself under my skin. Frustration at myself ebbs from me, flowing to him. His gaze darkens. Mine flits away and I swing my legs over the bed, needing to put distance between us.

"Raina—"

"Don't. Just don't." I stalk to the window, the sheet billowing behind me as I rush toward the table where my panties lie in a heap. Quickly, I tug them up my legs and as I straighten, his arms, strong and warm, circle around me.

"Listen to me, *bella*," he coaxes in that thick accent that heats my blood. My skin prickles as his warm breath fans over my bare shoulder. "Look at me, Raina." The command is a deep growl and even though I don't want to, I turn to face him.

"I just—"

His finger on my lips halts my words and he shakes his head. "Listen, I do want you. Last night was sensational. Feeling your body, touching your skin, tasting your cunt, that's what I want and need. This can work. I'll show you. This is something we both need. Our bodies, they fit together. You felt it. You saw it. Just give this agreement a chance. You'll learn more about yourself and I'll get to teach you." His words hold a vow that I know he'll make good on.

116

"So how will this work?" Lifting my chin, I regard him with an indignant stare. He reaches for my face, his knuckles brushing over my cheek lightly. The trail of his touch leaves goose bumps in its wake, but it's his eyes, the gentleness he looks at me with that slams into my chest, squeezing my heart. "Am I to be your possession?"

He nods then. "You are mine. I no longer care if you're known as the Lombardi principessa. This room, this home, it's yours. That bed"—he gestures to the four-poster we've just vacated—"is where you will sleep every night from now on. I did like having your body against mine. But I need you to remember one thing, Raina." He snaps his mocha orbs to mine. "We're not a couple. We're two consenting adults who fuck. Two people enjoying all the carnal pleasures we can. When you're in the office, you're my personal assistant. You'll be professional. You'll work for my brothers as well. When I bring you in here, you're my slut. Your holes are mine to do with as I please. And when you're not in this mansion, you're Raina Lombardi."

Nodding, I lift the sheet and step away from the intensity of our connection and grab my bra and the rest of my clothes. I don't know what the time is, but I know I should be heading home. "I'd like to leave. I'll be back for work in a few hours and I need to shower and get a change of clothes," I tell him without meeting his gaze, which is currently burning a hole in my back.

Once I'm dressed, he steps up behind me, his hands on my shoulders. "I'll have my driver take you home so you can pack and make sure your cousin knows you're safe with me. When you arrive back later, report to my office to sign the contract and then we'll be heading out to a meeting. It's time you saw the real aspects of my business."

With those final words, he releases me and guides me with his fingertips pressed lightly at the base of my spine.

As we weave our way through the large house, I hear sounds from the other side of the mansion. Just before we reach the door, Matteo, one of the younger brothers, comes stalking toward us.

"*Bella.*" He smirks, reaching for my hand and planting a chaste kiss on my knuckles. "So lovely to see you. Such a beautiful sight first thing in the morning."

"Thank you, Matteo. I was actually leaving. I'll be back later, though." My voice is barely audible and I clear my throat of all the emotions swirling through me. I wonder if he knows what his brother and I did.

"I can't wait till then. Franco, I've got the meeting with Russo set up today. He's not happy, but I have a feeling we'll need to be armed for this." He informs the man behind me and the tension that fills the open area is thick enough to cut with a knife.

"*Si, sono d'accordo.* I think we'll need to call in a favor." A silent nod passes between the men and then I'm ushered out the door. As I slip into the back seat of the car, Franco leans in and his lips feather mine. "Don't be late, Raina. Or you'll be punished." With that, I'm heading back to my apartment to pack a bag. Everything in my life has led me here. To this decision. To this life-altering change.

Shaking my head, I sit back and try to figure out just how I'm going to pull off working for a man with so many secrets. Some he hides so well, and others he doesn't know I've already uncovered.

13

FRANCO

"Was this part of your plan? To have your newest toy in the office? She will be a distraction, Franco." Matteo's right, but I can't not have her. After last night, all I can think about is her scent, her body, the way she felt beside me as she slept. "It's not a good idea to take her to Russo. If he sees her as your weakness—"

"She's not a weakness. I'm fine. What we have is an arrangement. Nothing more." Meeting those dark eyes that match mine, I can see the doubt in them. Always the level-headed one. Before we can continue our discussion, the subject of our heated exchange enters. Dressed in a flowing black dress that fits snugly at her waist and chest, she offers a small smile. As if she knew we were talking about her.

A soft blush appears on her cheeks and she dips her head without saying anything. The shy nature of this woman is the most alluring thing about her. I wonder if she's been made to feel small all her life, like she shouldn't even be here.

"I'm just telling you, brother. There are people out there who don't give a shit about hurting someone." His words are vague and I know it's for her benefit. I nod, sitting back, I regard him.

"Fine. We'll go alone." With that, he leaves the office without so much as a backward glance at Raina. "Come here." My tone is gruff and she quickly rises, rushing to my desk in her ballet flats. Sweet, innocent, beautiful. Three words that so aptly describe the blond beauty.

I'm enamored, but I know there can't be more than what I offered her. Granted, I've lusted after women before. But I've never felt the need to protect them the way I do her.

"I want you to stay here while Matteo and I head to the meeting. Something's come up and I'd rather you're safe. If you need anything, you can call me, but the people we're going to see are dangerous and I don't want you in the middle of the raging war we're about to start."

"What about you? Who keeps you safe?" Her question is adorable and I find myself chuckling. Me? I'm never safe. Not since I stepped up and into my father's shoes.

"Listen, *bella,* I'm a big boy. I can handle myself with these assholes. You, you're a waif, and you're mine. If they see you, they'll target you. Now, I want you to stay here. There's enough for you to do." I drop a stack of paperwork on the desk, which I need typed out. Contracts for new suppliers, as well as her own contract. "You'll need to read through and understand the document before you sign it. There's a non-disclosure agreement, which is imperative. After our six months are over, you move on, and you have enough money to do whatever you'd like to in life. You'll be able to study while you're at work when I'm out on business."

"Thank you. I..." Her gaze falls to the paper and she strokes it as if she's scared. Afraid of all the implications that are set out in a few measly white pages. The words on there are set in stone. Knowing she'll have to walk away sets her unease at an all-time high. She tries to hide it, but I can read women. Like an open book, the words she holds in her racing mind scream to me.

Swallowing deeply, I round my desk and close the distance between us. "Listen to me, Raina. You can always pull out. I still need a PA, but the other side of the contract isn't something you have to do if you feel you can't handle it. I hired you to help you get out of your *family obligations,* to help you. The sex"—I lean in and revel in the hitch of her breathing—"is just a perk."

"Brother, are you ready?" Gio's voice drags me from my intoxication with this beauty before me and I nod. It's time to do some business. To get that fucker out of my life. Russo has caused too much trouble. Granted, we've not had the best history, but it's time he learns who runs the West Coast.

"I am. Till later, *bella*." Turning, I head toward the door and find Giovanni's gaze flitting between me and the blonde who's captured my attention. My brothers aren't stupid. They can read through all my bullshit. And this is no different. Pushing emotions down is my forte. However, this sweet, innocent little girl is about to unravel everything. Something deep in my gut warns me. But who was I ever to listen to a warning.

"Ciao, bella." He salutes with one hand and I shut the door behind us. "I can see why you're growing attached to her, Franco." He smirks at me and I'm tempted to shut him up with a punch to the gut, but I pin him with a glare instead. "Don't let them see you like this. Pull your shit together or we're all going down." His tone has a warning dripping from it and I unbutton my suit jacket.

"Don't tell me how to run my life, Gio. I've done this a million times. As I said to Matteo this morning, she's a pet. Someone I can fuck my frustration out on. Nothing more."

With that, he drops the subject and hands me the contract for Russo.

It's been a long time coming. When my father was murdered by the same men he trusted, I vowed revenge. He doesn't realize I know he killed the older Moretti, and I intend to keep it that way until I've got him right where I want him. At the firing end of my gun. Then I'll watch as his brain is splattered along the wall. Crimson, such a pretty color.

Slipping into the back seat of the car, I find Matteo tapping away at his laptop. The IT guru of the three boys, my father always said he'd be the one to hack into any company one day and steal millions. And he has, pretty much.

We make our money from the drugs and weapons, but my brother, he likes to take from the rich and give to the poor. A modern-day Robin Hood. And the women seem to flutter to him like bees to honey, but somehow, when he's in a relationship, he's committed. He's always been a one-woman man. Like me.

Casting a glance at Gio, I take in my little brother. Born only a few minutes after Matteo, he is the baby. The manwhore as he likes to refer to himself. He's never without his Glock, a woman draped on his arm, and a cigarette hanging from his lips. When our father was killed, he took it the hardest. Went into a depression where we had to drag him from a drunken, drug-filled stupor and force him to get help.

We're all trained, and trained well. Matteo is lethal with his blades. Gio is glued to his gun. And me, I like using my hands. To feel the air slowly drain from someone's body. I know a few hundred ways to kill a man with a flick of my wrist. But I also have my pistol that used to be my father's, which has the family crest emblazoned on it.

The three of us are feared in circles all over the world. The Moretti name is infamous for making sure assholes are taken care of. The rest of us, those who worked for my father, they're as deadly as they are good-looking. Which works in our favor when we're wanting to get close to a mark.

In total, there are fifty men who are part of our family, our *cosca* as we like to call it, some I've known my whole life. And today, they'll go through a test of loyalty. To me, to my father, and to the Moretti name.

"We're almost here, sir," Lorenzo, my driver, informs us. Dragging my gaze toward the window, I take in the cars already parked and waiting. They're hidden from view, but I know they're there. If shit goes down, my men have my back. The gun wedged in the holster on my shoulder is evidence that this isn't a game. I'm ready to take men down, silent and deadly.

As soon as the car stops, I open the door and exit into the heat of the early afternoon. Our midday meeting has tension rolling through my body and when my brothers join me, I give a curt nod. A sign to let them know we're about to enter. Bringing backup was a good idea, but if Russo sees anything amiss, shit could go down and it won't be pretty.

Flanked by both Gio and Matteo, we head toward the large warehouse, which has two men standing guard at the entrance. Russo has never been one for subtlety. And his place of business is no different. Both guards open the double doors and when I step inside, Cristiano Russo walks up to me. "Ah, Franco, so good to see you." He leans in and kisses me on each cheek. The European way.

"I wish I could say the same to you," I retort hotly, but he chuckles. Turning, he stalks toward the office with four of his guards. The open plan room that is visible from the entrance is where he does all his underhanded deals. It's not the first time I've been here.

As I follow, both Matteo and Gio stay a step behind me, and as we enter the spacious office of my sworn enemy, he turns and offers me a seat. "Your brothers are looking good as well. Sit, please." He settles in his chair, which looks like a throne. "I want this sorted between us, no bad blood, as they say." The words sting, and he knows why. He's the reason I can never forgive myself for the choices I made. For the woman who was killed. I found her in a pool of blood in his bedroom. Not because she chose him, but because she didn't.

When he kidnapped her, held her against her will for two long months, I tried saving her. I was too late. I live with the guilt to this day. Murder is like passion, like addiction. It's addictive, but it's also poison. It can eat you from the inside until there's nothing left but an empty shell. A person you'll never recognize. All these years, I've allowed the blood of the men I've killed course like venom through my veins. The difference is that when I kill, it's not innocent, unsuspecting victims. They're all hardened criminals.

Just like me. Just like my family, and just like the man sitting in front of me.

Chucking the contract on his desk, I sit back and watch as he flips through it. All the terms and conditions state that my father owns the territory and the suppliers. No one else can work on this coastline without fear of them being killed.

"This doesn't work for me." He sits back, pushing the pages away as if they offend him.

"Like fuck it doesn't. You're not getting our region. My father worked long and hard to get the Moretti name all over the West Coast. If you're looking for land to steal you'll need to head to the east. I'm not giving you more than what's in that contract."

Pushing off the chair, I hear the click before I feel the cold metal poking my back. Guns are drawn. Matteo and Gio have guns on two of his four guards, and Russo's remaining two thugs have their guns on me. We've reached an impasse, but there's no way I'm stepping down and allowing this piece of filth anywhere near my home or my woman. They can kill me first. The thought of Rai being taken by Russo has rage flaring like a wildfire in my blood, threatening to consume me.

"Make no mistake, Franco, I will get what I want. I always do." He rises, rounding his desk and closing the distance between us. We're both the same age, both our fathers' heirs to the riches they've left behind, but only one of us can rule at a time. I took the helm, he stepped back. Now that we're making more money than they thought was possible, they're forcing our hand.

Well, fuck it. "Cristiano fucking Russo, listen, and listen well. You're welcome to shoot me right now, but I'll never give up, not without a fight. So the only way you'll get your hands on my father's deeds is if your boys here put some metal straight into my heart and you let me bleed all over your pretty white carpet."

"Don't tempt me, Moretti, I'm not averse to having some red in my life. In fact, I love seeing blood all over my hands. It's a pity you don't, always trying to be the good guy." He chuckles, turning away from me, he gestures with his hand for his men to stand down and they obey.

"There's nothing wrong with being the good guy. You need to learn your place. If something happens to me, you know they'll come down on you like a fucking hurricane wiping away everything in its path. And I know the reason you didn't splatter my brain all over your expensive carpet is because you know it as well as I do. Your fancy lifestyle here in the US will be a thing of the past, and you know why? Because respect is earned, not bought."

"Get out. Take your contract. I don't want it," he spits at me and I can't help the smirk. He knows I'm right. Heads will roll if something were to happen to me or my brothers.

"My sovereignty over the West Coast will never die, even if I do. It's my territory, Cristiano, remember that." With my warning in place, I turn to walk out of his office, but not before he gets the last word in.

"And my territory is right here, behind you. Watch your back, Franco. Not everything is as it seems."

I don't respond because I know exactly what he means. I'm not stupid. I've done my homework. All I need to do now is keep one woman safe. It's not difficult. I failed once. I won't do it again.

14

RAINA

Packing this morning was easy. I didn't have much that I wanted to bring along. Also, I would be here temporarily. If I needed anything, I'm sure I'd be free to leave. As soon as the car pulls up to the house, Franco's driver exits the vehicle and makes his way to my side. Opening the door for me, he proffers his hand.

"Thank you." When I smile up at him, it's as if he knows why I'm here, not only to work for the Morettis, but to be whatever Franco wants me to be.

Yet, he doesn't say a word, only escorts me to the door where the housekeeper is waiting with a friendly smile.

"Ciao, I'm Donatella." Her accent is thick, more so than any of the brothers'. "I take you to your room," she informs me before turning to head up the sweeping staircase. The house is silent, without so much as a sound coming from the kitchen or even the grounds outside.

There's a long hallway that we meander down at a slow pace and I notice Donatella's limp. Once we pass by four doors, she stops at the fifth and pushes it open.

"If you need something, I'm in kitchen," she once again

speaks in her broken English and then leaves me to enter the incredible suite I've been offered.

It's an ultra-modern space with a king-sized four-poster bed. With a jet-black chest of drawers and the walls painted an off-white, it's almost clinical, but the enormous deep red rug that covers most of the floor adds warmth. The bedding, with white and silver, adorns the mattress. To the left of the entrance is a walk-in closet with enough room for a small army, and beside that, hidden behind two large mirrors, is a large en-suite.

My cell ringing drags me from the memories of what happened last night, and all the pleasure Franco bestowed on my wanton body. As I pull the phone from my purse, I swipe my thumb to answer, but I hear my cousin before I can say *hello.*

"How is the mansion? Sitting at the pool with cocktails?"

"You're so frustrating," I retort while rolling my eyes at her. "I'm actually in my new bedroom. It's incredible, Cali." Awe in my voice is evident and I flop onto the bed. Staring up at the ceiling, I hear her take a deep breath.

"I can't believe you're living with Franco. Like in the same house. Are you two...?" She allows the question to taper off, hanging like a lead weight between us.

"No, we're just working. He needs me here. I... I've signed the contract for the six months. It will give me the stability I need. Away from Andrea." She knows how I feel about my brother. About the way he handles our finances and rules over us with an ironclad fist.

Sighing, she responds, her voice dropping, "I'm sorry, Rai. He's an asshole. Soon I'll be gone. The contract I told you I got offered, I signed this morning. I'm going to be modeling again soon. I can't wait to get away from your ass face brother." She sighs, then asks, "Do you still get alone time? I mean, can we go to dinner or something?"

"Of course, babe. Franco isn't locking me up in a cage." As soon as the words fall from my lips, the image presents itself. Me in a collar, kneeling in a cage with him commanding me to touch myself.

A deep rumble comes from the doorway and I jolt upright. The man himself leans on the doorjamb, his shirt hugging impeccable toned shoulders.

"I have to go," I murmur into the phone, and before Calista can respond, I hang up.

"A cage? I didn't think you'd be into that sort of thing, but if you're willing, so am I," he quips, his tone thick with desire. Dripping over me, instilling that hunger that he seems to ignite deep in my veins.

"I was... I mean... my cousin was worried." Stumbling over my words, I push off the bed and stand.

"Of course. Do you like the room? I know this isn't the most conventional arrangement, but..." His eyes take in the room and when they land on me again, there's something that's hidden in those dark depths. "I'd like to make this work." The way he voices those words, it feels like *more*. Just so much more than what he said he wants and I wonder if he would ever love. Perhaps not me specifically, but anyone.

That brings my mind to his past. Has he lost someone before? Is that why he's so opposed to it? Or is it really his lifestyle that's got him pushing the thought of being with anyone away.

"I'm here, Franco. I agreed and signed. I'm not leaving until you tell me otherwise. Sometimes, you need to let go of past hurts to find happiness."

I don't know where my courage comes from, but once again, I notice how his gaze hardens. "I'll be back later.

Make yourself comfortable." With that, he turns on his heel and stalks out of the room, slamming the door behind him. Something has hurt that man, and I intend to find out what it is.

THE KITCHEN IS IMMACULATE. IT'S BEEN AN HOUR SINCE FRANCO stormed out of the bedroom, leaving me wondering how to get into his mind. "Hello." Spinning around, I find Gio sitting on a chair at the table. He's got his laptop in front of him and a cigarette hanging from his full lips.

"I didn't know anyone was in here. I'm sorry."

"Stay, I don't mind the company. I'm finishing up some work." He gestures to the chair opposite him, which I slide into. His eyes, a rich chestnut color, bore into me as he drags his gaze from my face down to my chest. For a moment, his stare settles on my breasts, and when I blink, he's turned away, focusing on the screen in front of him. "Did you want dinner? There are some leftovers in the fridge. Ginnie made some lasagna. She's a great cook, so I'm sure it's good." He speaks almost as if it's a rehearsed speech. I wonder if he knows what his brother is into. What he does.

"Thank you. I thought Franco—"

"He's not here. He left an hour ago," he informs me with a wave of his hand, the white smoke creating intricate patterns in the air around him.

"Oh." My voice cracks on the word, which has his eyes snapping up to mine. Before he can see the hurt that must be so clear on my face, I push up and head to the large steel refrigerator in the corner of the incredible kitchen. Opening the door, I find it fully stocked with food enough for an army. The container labelled with lasagna on the lid sits glaring at me, but I find my appetite gone.

"Listen, *bella,* he's a difficult man. I know this, but when he cares for someone, he has this tendency to push people away." Gio's voice has me turning to face him. The light of the fridge shines into the room and illuminates it.

"I don't understand, to be honest. I've been pushed away all my life. I signed the contract in the hope that I'll—"

"You can't change him. You can't help him. It's who he is. Don't take it personally. He's like that with everyone. Sometimes, he even pushes us away."

"What happened to him?" I question, shutting the refrigerator and closing the distance between us as I settle in the chair again. I want to know more about the man who has embedded himself inside me.

"It's not my story to tell, *bella,* but just know that he pushes people away for a reason. Our life"—he glances away, looking at something on the screen before he brings those brown pools back to mine—"it's dangerous and all the people we care about could get hurt in the blink of an eye."

"Then why not just... I don't know... stop?" It's then that Giovanni chuckles. His laugh is musical, deep and rough. He's handsome. The creases at the edge of his eyes make him look older than he is, and his full lips press against white teeth. I thought he was handsome when he's serious, but his smile lights up his face in such a way that he almost looks like a painting. Like you want to freeze time just to look at it.

"*Sei divertente.* Funny girl," he points at me with long, slender fingers. "The only way out is if we're buried six feet under, Raina." A shudder races through me at his warning. "It's our life."

"It's not a life, it's a death sentence." My vehement words earn me another chuckle and he shuts the lid of his laptop, bathing us in darkness. A sliver of light from the new moon is all that illuminates us.

"A death sentence that we're born into," he affirms with a nod and pushes up from the table. The chair scrapes across the tiles and he positions it back under the table. "Remember, *caro*"—the Italian word for darling drips seductively from his lips—"you can't change the stripes of a tiger. All you can do is learn to appreciate them."

He turns then and saunters out of the kitchen with my gaze following each confident step. Giovanni is dangerous in his own way, oozing confidence, sexual prowess, and I know he has the ability to bring any woman he wants to her knees and that makes me worry about my cousin. I know they've been seeing each other, and something tells me she's going to fall head over heels for the man who I find myself gaping at.

"Something wrong?" Franco's voice drags me from my thoughts. He's standing in the doorway, watching me. The silvery light casts his face in a glow that makes him look ethereal.

"No, I came down to find some dinner, but ended up chatting to Gio for a little while. He just left." He nods, stepping farther into the shadows.

"Come." Offering a hand, he waits until I slip mine into his. "I must apologize for earlier," he states matter-of-factly, as if it was a misunderstanding that he stormed out of the room, leaving me reeling. As we make our way down a long hallway, I realize we must be going to his personal suite. My heart rate spikes as we stop at what I'm guessing is the entrance to his bedroom. He's been silent all the way, and it's only when he opens the door and allows me to step inside that I notice what he's done. A small table at the window with two candles shimmering against the glass, a place setting on either side, and a bottle of red wine with two glasses await.

The room itself is dark, a contrast to the one I'm meant to be staying in. The walls are a dark brown, with wooden paneling and one filled with books, old books, that remind me of my father's library. The only word I can think to best describe the bed is humungous. It's a four-poster, and I'm certain he enjoys making full use of them by tying his submissives to them.

"What's this?"

"My apology." He stalks by me, pulling out a chair. "This is my room." He gestures for me to sit. Once I'm settled, he slips into the seat opposite and lifts the bottle, pouring the red liquid into the crystal goblets. The rich scent of Merlot hits my nostrils and I inhale deeply, enjoying the smell of the wine.

"You know"—I lift the glass to my lips, taking a long sip before continuing—"I'd much prefer you either an asshole or not. Your current mood swings are difficult to get a handle on. As if I'm watching a tennis match. Jekyll and Hyde."

He regards me silently for a moment and I take another long gulp of the alcohol, which seeps into my bloodstream. My body is buzzing from an empty stomach and almost a full glass of wine.

"Perhaps, act the asshole, so when I walk away, it will be less traumatic." It seems my mouth has a mind of its own because I can't stop it from spewing shit and the dark glare Franco pins me with has my body both trembling and quivering.

"So you want me to act like an asshole toward you?" His head tips to the side. He regards me with a look filled with curiosity. The energy in the room is palpable. Thick and unyielding, and it leaves me speechless. "Rai, I told you that's who I am. And if you listen to my brother, you'll know it's not you I show that side to, it's everyone."

"Why do you push people away? He told me you've been hurt before. Is it because you're afraid to love some-one?" I should shut up. I shouldn't taunt him or anger him, but I can't help myself. My stubborn pride always gets the better of me and I watch as his face turns from gentle inquisitiveness to something akin to rage. But he doesn't direct it at me. Ice fills the space between us as he gently sets his glass down. He pushes up from the chair and rounds the table toward me.

"Stand." Immediately, I find myself obeying his order. "Turn around." I face the window, with his heat on my back. The tense energy that simmers behind me causes me to shudder and he hasn't even touched me yet.

In one swift move, he rips my yoga pants down my legs and allows me to step out of them. With his one foot, he kicks mine apart. Spreading me for him. A firm hand pushes me forward and I have to hold on to the window to keep from stumbling. I'm bent at the waist, wearing nothing but a tank top.

He doesn't comment on the fact that I have no panties on. Instead, I hear the shuffle of his clothes, but I don't dare turn to look at what he's doing. Silence falls around us and I watch the cars on the highway in the distance. Movement behind me sends my senses into overdrive as he reaches in front of me and ties a material over my eyes. In an instant, my world is black.

For a long while, I stand there, feeling the heat of his gaze as it travels over me. The soft cotton of my top falls away when he slices it from my body with the steak knife. I'm only guessing that's what he used because I can't hear anything else being shifted.

"Franco." My voice is tentative, but he doesn't answer me. Instead, the cold liquid of what I assume is the red wine trails from my neck down my back and trickles between my ass cheeks. A shiver races through me and goose bumps rise on every inch of my skin. I await more, but it never comes because his mouth is on me in an instant.

He licks and nips at the flesh between my thighs, lapping at the wine and my arousal mixing on his tongue. A swat on my ass has me yelping. Another and another is rained down on my skin. His hands spread me open obscenely and I can't stop the heat, the blush that I know is clear on my cheeks.

His tongue darts into my forbidden puckered entrance, which sends me spiraling. The need to orgasm taunts me. But he's an expert at this and keeps me on edge. Between his tongue lapping at me, teasing my ass, and nibbling on my clit, my nails attempt to dig into the window, but all I do is claw at the slippery surface.

My knees tremble and I don't know how much longer I can hold on. "If you come, I'll punish you, *bella*. Make no mistake," he warns and I bite my lip to keep from coming too soon, before he orders me to.

Another swat and another. More. I want to ask him for more, but words fail me. As soon as it started, he stops. I'm left trembling as I hear the clink of a belt buckle and I know I'm in for it.

"You want love? You want a sweet relationship where I buy you flowers?" he questions and I shake my head because to be honest, I don't want that. I've never been fond of flowers. Yes, perhaps I wanted love, but this... this violent passion he's giving me is so much more. It sets me alight. "Answer me," he commands and with it the leather of the belt bites into the soft flesh of my ass.

"NO!" I cry out. The pain, ignites every nerve in my body. The desire flares to life like a raging inferno.

"Count," he bites out through clenched teeth and I do.

"One." Swat. "Two." My body is electric. My clit throbs. My orgasm is hanging heavy, threatening to detonate me. "Three, four." My voice is barely audible. My skin burns with every bite, but when he drops the belt and plunges his cock inside me, my body shudders and my orgasm rears, waiting for the order. The command.

"I'll give you want you want, *bella,* but be warned. I'm always going to be an asshole. I'm always going to hurt you. Keep your heart locked away because I will break it if you give it to me." He hisses as his hips buck into me. His hands reach for my breasts. My nipples are hardened peaks as he twists them painfully. The pain and pleasure mixing, swirling together in a vortex of intensity I've only ever felt last night when he took me, grips me, and when he leans in and whispers in my ear, "Give it to me. Give me your body, Raina," I let go. My body quivers, pulses, squeezes, and sucks his cock deeper, needing it in every corner of me. He's not only fucking my body, he's fucking my mind even though he's warned me against it.

In that moment.

I give him the one thing I know he will break.

My heart.

15

FRANCO

"**Y**ou had no right to tell her anything about me," I grunt at my brother, who sits in the office chair like he owns the goddamn place. "She is an employee, nothing more."

Even as I say the words, I know they're a lie. It's been almost a week after I fucked her against the window in my bedroom. That night, all I wanted to hide from her, everything I held dear, fell away. With my cock inside her so deep it felt as if I'd burrowed my way into her soul and she into mine. It's a mistake. It's going to be my downfall, but I'm spiraling. There's no way to stop it. I'm falling for her.

Since then, I've been professional. I haven't touched her. She's slept in the guest room because I told her to. I needed space. A whole fucking week of not being inside her is driving me crazy. Today the shipment of weapons arrives and I need a clear head. This job will either make us or break us in this city, and if I'm going to get my revenge on that asshole, I need to be on top of shit, not sitting here worried about a little blonde who somehow has me by the balls.

Raking my fingers through my hair, I settle on my

expensive leather office chair and watch Gio's smoke rings fill my office.

"Franco, you're going to have to choose. Either you let her go, or you make her part of the family. You tell her everything." He's right. But the truth will have her running for the hills. I've already gotten myself too deep into this. If she found out why she's really here, I don't think she'll ever want to see me again.

Perhaps that's the way to go. Maybe if she's the one walking away, I can get over this shit. These emotions that seem to steal every thought. Before I can decide, the door swings open and she walks in. Looking radiant in a black-and-white dress that stops at her knees. Her delicate feet in those flats she prefers over heels and her long blond waves are sleeked straight and hang down to the middle of her back.

"Good morning," she greets, her gaze flitting between Gio and me.

"It's our gorgeous girl." My brother turns on the charm and I know he's trying to irk me by doing it. Her blush is evident, but it's her eyes that give her away. They're pinned on mine. Questions dance in them, ones I can't give her answers to, unless I want her even deeper in this shit than she already is.

Do I want that? Can I give her the secrets I hold dear to me? Will she forgive me if she finds out?

"I want you to set up a meeting today at three with your brother," I inform her and she nods. My brother's gaze snaps to mine. With one look, he asks me *are you going to tell her?* But I don't answer. Instead, I turn to my computer and focus on work. Ordering more coke from our Colombian supplier, I hit send on the email and wait for the response I know will be immediate. Carlos doesn't disappoint when he agrees to the price, the date of delivery, and the special request I've included.

———

Stepping into the room, I find Andrea sitting at the conference table. "Mr. Moretti." He rises, offering a hand. I shake, but I can feel the anxiety pulsating off him. He knows why he's here, but I won't give away all my cards. He'll need to work for them.

I know secrets about this asshole that can send him away for years. Perhaps even a lifetime. The door opens and his sister walks in with the tray that has the cafetière and cups. "Thank you, Raina. That will be all," I murmur as she regards me with a smile. Her gaze flits to her brother, but she doesn't award him with a greeting. Instead, she turns and walks out of the room.

"She seems happy here," he remarks with a hint of frustration.

"Why wouldn't she be?" Tipping my head to the side, I regard him quizzically. When he shakes his head, anger races through me. His lies will one day catch up to him, and when they do, I'll be the one who will avenge Raina's name.

"No reason. What can I do for you?"

"Russo." The name falls easily with venom and his gaze darts to mine in surprise. The emotions this asshole tries to hide are written clearly on his face. He'll never be one of us, as much as he's tried.

"What about it?"

"It? Russo is the name of the man who is responsible for both our fathers' deaths. Surely you know this?" Lifting the mug, I take a sip of the coffee, savoring the thick sludge. Caffeine races through my veins as I watch him squirm.

When Matteo brought the paperwork to me, I knew I

had to do this. I had to see if this man was the snake we suspect him to be. As he sits in the chair, I can almost see him slithering through the responses.

No backbone.

No respect.

Just a piece of filth.

"I... There wasn't any confirmation on who did it," he mumbles, then meets my stare. "Your father was shot as well?" he questions, and I nod. "And you believe this... Russo person was responsible?"

I want to round this table and choke him. I want to grip his neck and slowly hear the choked breaths of the air draining from his lungs. The thought makes me smile. "Oh, I know he was, it's a fact, not a suspicion. You see, Mr. Lombardi, I have connections everywhere. Both on the West Coast, as well as the East. Very dangerous men know about Cristiano Russo and they're not happy with the way things have been playing out," I speak clearly, but my voice is low, filled with a warning. I don't mention who Cristiano is to me. I hardly ever acknowledge the bastard as family.

For Raina's sake, I hope he tells me the truth and confesses. I'm doing this for her, so I don't have to tell her about the man she's grown up with as a brother. But he's not smart. He's far from it, in fact, because he doesn't take the bait.

"Well, I'm not sure who he is, but if I hear anything around the bar, I'll let you know." He sips the coffee his sister set down for him and winces at the heat. The image of torturing him with scalding hot liquid makes me smile.

Yes, I'm a bad person, evil, in fact. I hurt people. I enjoy it. And this piece of scum sitting at my table deserves so much more.

Once again, the door flies open and right on time Gio stalks into the room. "Mr. Lombardi, apologies for interrupting, but this is urgent." My brother sets the documents on the table in front of me and I nod.

"Thank you, Gio. I'll be done in a few moments. I'm sure Andrea has important things to catch up on. Don't you?" We both settle our stares on the man who seems to now be fumbling for an answer. Easy prey. He nods. Gulps down the coffee that I know must still be warm and I feel the buzz inside. I get it every time I'm about to torture someone.

The first time I felt it was when I was thirteen. My father taught me how to slice a man's fingers from his hand. It was euphoric. Like sex, violent, yet passionate. Intoxicating. It was something I craved. Like a hit of heroin to the vein. Ever since then, I've been addicted to it.

"I've got some deliveries coming for the bar. I'm sorry I couldn't help you find this Russo character. If I do hear anything or see anything untoward, I'll definitely let you know, Franco." He uses my first name like we're friends. We're not. Far from it.

If he were on fire in front of me, I wouldn't piss on him. In fact, I may even be the one to light the match. "Of course." My smile is as fake as this asshole. Offering him my hand, we shake, and Gio escorts him out. Pushing the button on the intercom, I wait for her sweet voice to filter through.

"Franco?"

"Come in here right now." My order is gruff, more than I intend it, and I'm sure she thinks she's in trouble. I wouldn't mind bending her over this table and making her scream, but there are more serious matters for her to learn about.

Gio and Matteo were right. If I want this woman, I'm going to need to be honest with her. When she enters the room, her big blue eyes meet mine, filled with concern. "Is there a problem?" Shaking my head, I gesture at the chair and rise from my own. Once she's seated, I stroll to the door and lock it.

"I need to bring you deeper into this than I wanted to," I start, slipping back into my seat. Her scent fills the room, sweetness and innocence with a bite of dark. There's an animal inside this girl that I want to let loose and have her devour me.

"I thought I was already in too deep?" The concern in her tone is warranted. This was the last thing I wanted. But I've made a choice.

"I need you to listen to me. It's about your father. It's about something I did." Meeting her gaze, I reach for her hand, which she gives me without a flinch. "I know who murdered your father." The words are out before I can hold them back.

There's no other way to do this, so I inhale a deep breath and let the story flow from me.

"It was the first time I did something that could have been handled differently. My father had found out that Mr. Lombardi senior was stealing money from him. Your father did our taxes for a while, a long while. Since before you were born."

She nods as if she knew this. She doesn't seem surprised and I stop, watching her with my brows furrowed.

"You're telling me things I've known for a long time, Franco. My father wasn't above the law. I've seen things, heard things." She shrugs and meets my gaze again.

"But—"

"I didn't know it was you when you first walked into the bar that night, and after our first night, that's when I realized it really was you." She's not making any sense now. The first time I saw Raina was the night in the bar when I met with her brother. There's no way she's seen me before.

"Raina, I think you're confused."

"No." She shakes her head with a small smile. "There were photos in my father's office. I found them the first time when I was sixteen," she continues, but I'm still left confused. "My father kept them because he needed insurance from what he was doing, I guess. But there was one photo in particular. It didn't have a name scribbled on it like the others. It was of a young man, perhaps in his early twenties. At least, that's what he looked like. With dark hair and eyes. Handsome. Dangerous-looking."

A small grin along with her cheeks darkening make me tip my head to the side as I tug her hand to get her to look at me. "So this dangerous, handsome stranger, did you perhaps fantasize about him?" The question has her gaze darting up in surprise, but she nods shyly.

"Yes." The word is a soft whisper. Almost too quiet to catch, but I am so attuned to her, I hear everything. Even if she doesn't utter it. She's a part of me now and I'll never let that go.

"And tell me, Raina. What was it that you thought about when you saw the photo?"

"The man intrigued me. I stole the photo from my dad. He never noticed. I suppose that's when it started…" Her words taper off and she sits quietly, her hand in mine. Nothing could have prepared me for what came out of her mouth next. "It was you." Lifting big blue eyes to meet mine, she smirks. It's playful, sexy, and downright devilish.

"Me?"

"Yes, Dad had documents with all the Nostra in Los Angeles. When your father was at my house one day, I noticed the similarities. It was then that I found out he had three sons. You, Gio, and Matteo. I didn't know your names, but he spoke of you often in that meeting."

"And you fantasized about me? I mean…"

She nods then. Her teeth pull her plump lower lip between them and she bites down. It must be painful because she winces slightly.

"Tell me, *bella*," I lean in and murmur in her ear, "What is it that you thought about?"

Her breathing hitches and her chest rises and falls with each breath. Her nipples harden behind the soft material of her blouse and bra, and I can tell when she rubs her thighs together. When she doesn't answer, I continue provoking her.

"Did you think about this?" I run my fingers up her thigh. Its featherlight. Tickling, teasing, taunting. Her eyes flutter closed, and her lips part. Soft, heated breaths fall from her and I want to swallow each one. They're mine. I own her, every part of her. Since she was sixteen, touching her cunt looking at my photo.

"Yes." The word escapes on a moan.

"And did you think about this?" My hand finds the wet, heated spot between her thighs and her head drops back. "Look at me." Leisurely, she lifts her head and the hot stare she pins me with is enough for me to lose all my fucking restraint. "Do you want to fuck a man who killed someone in cold blood? Someone you loved." The question jolts her back to reality. "You don't know, do you?"

"Know what?"

"Your father, his death…" I can't continue. She'll run and I don't want her to, but before I can say anything more or find the words to explain, her body stills. As if ice has just run through her veins.

"What?"

Sighing, I sit back but keep my hand on her thigh, needing the connection. "There's a man I've been trying to take down for a long time. Cristiano Russo. The same one we met with earlier today. I've given him an out, which I didn't think he'd accept. And I was right. We used to be close, like brothers. But it's all changed. Things don't always work out how we think they will."

I glance at her, hoping she'll realize what I'm talking about. It's all gone to shit. At least that's what it feels like. When I knew I'd have to one day look into the eyes of the Lombardi siblings and tell them the truth about their father.

"He set up a meeting at his warehouse on the outskirts of San Diego. It was a bust. When I walked into the warehouse, there were men inside waiting for me. Between my father and yours, with both my brothers flanking me, we managed to get out. But before we got to the car, we found your father. He was badly injured."

Shutting my eyes, I recall that night like it was yesterday. Seeing Mr. Lombardi lying on the ground, I knew it was his doing. He called them before we arrived and warned them. Working both sides like he was, it could only be a matter of time before he saw his end.

"He confessed, while he bled out. He was in on the setup to help Russo kill my father. He knew he was done. That's when he mentioned your name. You and your cousin. That night, I allowed anger to overtake me. In the moment I lifted my gun and pulled the trigger, I didn't see Cristiano behind me a gun pointed at my father with his finger on the trigger. Two shots were fired and one promise was made that night."

Silence surrounds us. Her anger, confusion, and rage simmer just below the surface as she regards me. Taking in what I've just told her. The memory of that night when I promised a dying man I'd find his daughter and keep her safe plays in my mind every day. That was the night he gurgled the truth about his son. About Andrea.

I don't move.

I don't even dare breathe.

"You killed him?" Her voice is that of a little girl. A teenager who lost her father. An innocent daughter who lost her hero. I can't find words, so I nod. And when her eyes meet mine, I see it. Shimmering in her bright blue eyes is her heart, cracking with each word, every memory, and it's all my fault.

I warned her. I told her I'd hurt her, break her heart. And I did.

16

RAINA

It's surreal when you're face to face with a killer. It's something I could never describe because I couldn't give it justice with words. Knowing your father was murdered in cold blood is one thing, but when you're the one in love with his killer. That's another thing completely.

Glancing at him, I realize one thing. He's dangerous and deadly, but it makes me want him even more.

He doesn't move. I know he's waiting for the tirade. For the anger. For everything I should be giving him. But I can't. I don't. I knew what my father had done. So as I look at Franco, I see the guilt in his dark eyes, but it's not guilt over killing my father.

No.

That would be fruitless.

It's remorse over hurting me. Shaking my head, I pull my hand from his and he reluctantly lets me go. Turning, I head toward the floor-to-ceiling windows that overlook the city. "You know, there were times when I wondered how he died. I wondered who the man was behind the gun. It played on my mind day and night. And you know what I did during those moments, hours, minutes?"

He's silent, but I don't turn to him. I can't look at him as I voice the next words. As I admit that I'm not angry. Perhaps a little hurt, but not angry.

"I lay in my bed, I looked at the photo of the stranger, and I imagined it was him. I pictured his strong hands holding a black Glock, or perhaps a handgun with a silencer, and I saw his fingers press the trigger. I heard the shot. It echoed through my mind every night. The sound would ricochet around me and the strange thing was, that was when I realized how fucked up I am."

"What?" He rasps the question and I place a hand on the glass, recalling those nights alone. Those nights when I found my father's secrets. When I learned the man I called daddy wasn't what he said he was. When I learned that secrets and lies were what broke my family apart.

"It's true. I learned that I wasn't his daughter. Because the only thing I thought of, the only thing I did every night after, even before my father's death, was think of you. I'd fallen for a stranger in a photo. You gave me my first real orgasm without even touching me. You showed me a part of me I didn't know I had, you ripped it from the cold darkness where it hid and you gave it light."

He's behind me then. He moved so swiftly, I didn't hear him approach. But his body is behind mine in an instant. "Raina." He caresses my name in his thick accent. Dripping confusion and hunger. "What are you talking about?"

"I..." My words fall short because I can't admit it. I can't tell him I sought him out but couldn't find him. I didn't know his name, and I couldn't find any information in my father's documents. I'd waited too long after his death. When I went into his study, everything was gone. The police had taken it all. And so, my stranger was gone.

"Can you feel this?" He strokes my arm. It's a gentle, almost tentative touch. Sweet. Soft. Different to how he normally touches me. I nod. "Not my fingers, *bella,*" he murmurs against my neck and I dip my head to the side to allow him access to the sensitive flesh. "This tethered connection. It's... *intossicante,*" he murmurs.

"What?"

"Intoxicating, Raina." His lips plant a soft kiss on my nape. "That's what you are to me. I can't deny myself you. You're my addiction. A wicked sin I could never pray for salvation for taking and enjoying. I won't survive this life without a shot of you to my veins every day." His words are filled with emotion, affection, something deeper than we both agreed to. Something I wanted, but he couldn't give.

As I turn in his arms, I regard him. I see it swimming in those mocha pools. His eyes remind me of those espresso shots he loves to drink. Deep, dark, and bottomless.

"I'm not leaving. I can't. I know you told me I shouldn't do this, but as they say, the heart wants what it does. And mine..." I lean in, my lips on the scruff of his jaw and I revel in the way it scrapes along my cheek. "My heart wants yours."

It's been two weeks, two long fucking weeks, and he hasn't touched me again. I've slept in the guest room, far from him. He told me he needed to focus on work, but I know he's lying. I saw it in his eyes. The afternoon I told him I wanted him, he did what Gio said he'd do. Pushed me away. Only, I don't believe his cold shoulder act. It was blatantly clear in his eyes when he looked at me there was so much emotion shining in them. It knocked me breathless.

Even when I knew he'd hide it, I didn't expect him to just block me out completely. At work, he's been attentive but professional. When the sun sets, he stalks out of the office and I don't see him again until the next morning. At first, I thought he had someone else, that he was leaving and visiting another woman, but when I stumbled upon him in the gym in the basement one night, I realized he'd been spending his hours working out.

After a chat with Matteo, he admitted that Franco wasn't, in fact, seeing other women, and he'd only ever seen his brother act so strangely once. And that was when he was with his ex. I still don't know what happened to her. Something tells me I'm better off not having that information divulged to me.

Sitting back, I sip the cocktail in front of me, with my mind racing through Franco leaving this morning for New York. He was gone before I had a moment to process anything. With a chaste kiss on my forehead, he was gone. To be honest, it stung, and I sat for most of the day wondering why he couldn't just give in to his feelings and admit it.

At least, he could to me. Even if he didn't want his brothers to know. Not that they'd have a problem since I've become like part of the family. The same family he told me holds his heart. Questions, confusion, and no answers, taunt me as I drink the blue concoction of alcohol my cousin insisted on buying me.

"Are you going to sit and mope all night?" Casting a glance at Calista, I shrug.

"I'm not moping. I just find it really strange that a man who is nearly forty is so afraid of being honest with his feelings and emotions." Frustration is evident in my tone.

"I think he's planning to propose," my best friend, Adria, says, ever the positive one. Needing a happily ever after. Although I've always wanted one too, I was honest when I told him I just wanted him. Even if he wasn't offering me a ring, I needed him. The ache in my chest is too much, and I shake my head to clear the thoughts of him walking away and find two sets of eyes on me.

"He won't propose. I just need to give him space. He needs it. He just can't love." Even as the words fall from my mouth, the ache in my chest tightens, gripping that useless muscle that beats, at the moment, only for him.

"So you're just going to give up your life for a man who blatantly told you he can't love you?" My cousin's glare is incredulous. So is my best friend's. They're looking at me like I've lost my mind, and I think I have. Only, they don't know the whole story. I do. If I told my cousin what Andrea did, she'd never forgive him. It was his fault my father was killed by Franco. Only, it was my father who killed the older Moretti by his betrayal of a life-long client. Someone who'd put their trust in him.

Jesus, this is like a goddamn soap opera. All I wanted was a normal life. I know Franco vowed to tell me the whole truth when he got back, but with all that he's already told me, I have too many suspicions racing through my head. I can't ask Gio because he wouldn't go against his brother's wishes and say anything, so I wait.

"Listen to me, Rai." Adria reaches for my hand and stares at me. "If this is the man you want, don't let us tell you what to do. But be careful. You know the Nostra are dangerous. Your father got involved with them and look where he is now. That was his choice to do. I don't know all the details, but this is something you need to decide. Nobody can tell you what's right or wrong. It's all you."

I nod, understanding what she means, but as much as I do get it, they need to know the whole story.

Only, I don't know if I should be the one to tell them.

"There's so much you both don't know." My gaze implores them both and with that, they regard me through narrowed gazes. "So many goddamn secrets and it pisses me off that we grew up around this shit. With all these dangerous people, but there are things that he told me about my father." I murmur the last few words because even when he told me, I found it a difficult pill to swallow.

"Then tell us, Rai," my best friend asks and I take a deep lungful of air, hoping it will give me the confidence to admit the mistakes of our families. Before I can, a man dressed in exquisite Armani steps up to our table with the bravado of only a member of the Nostra can.

"Ladies." The quirk of his mouth lifts into a smirk, and it's then that I notice the two men flanking him. A flick of his fingers commands me to shift so he can sink into the bench seat beside me. The two bodyguards, at least that's what I think they are, step closer to the table, prohibiting us from leaving. We're trapped.

"Who are you?" He leans back, his arm curling around my shoulders as he pulls me closer. The thick scent of an expensive, spicy cologne invades my nostrils. The smell is familiar and I wrack my brain trying to figure out when or where I've come across it before.

"I, my sweet Raina, am Cristiano. I'm sure you remember me. Don't you?" he whispers in my ear and the memory hits me square in the chest. "I think it will stay our little secret," he murmurs quietly. *It's him. Shit.* "My two friends over here, Luciano and Armand, they're just here to make sure you pretty ladies don't cause a scene." His fingertips trace circles over my bare shoulder, which cause me to shudder. His dark, slicked back hair, tanned skin, and thick Italian accent tell me he knows Franco from back home.

"What do you want?"

He smiles then. If he wasn't scaring me, I'd have said it was a handsome smile. He pins me with the most intense green eyes I've ever seen that remind me of Chartreuse.

Almost luminous. And against his olive skin tone, he could easily pass as a model for GQ. The expensive suit is tailor made because when he moves it hugs his torso perfectly.

"You're going to be visiting my home for a little while, and since you've got these lovely ladies with you, they might as well come too. We can have a little party." His voice drops on the last few words and the rasp of hunger is clear.

"Franco—"

"Will know where you are. You see, he owes me, and I'm here to collect." The corner of his full pink lips lifts into a perfect sinister smirk that has fear slowly dripping into my bloodstream as if I'd taken a shot of alcohol.

"Listen, I think you're making a—"

My words are cut off when I feel the barrel of cold metal pressed against my ribs. "Does this feel like I'm making a mistake, *tesoro*?" The way he murmurs *sweetheart* in his language stirs anxiety in my belly and I can't find words to respond. Instead, I shake my head and meet my cousin's blue eyes. Fear dances in them and I nod. Hoping she'll play along so we don't get hurt.

When I was accosted in the nightclub almost three weeks ago, Franco came to my rescue, but this time, I don't think he will. He's away on business in New York for two days with Matteo, leaving only Gio here. But of course, work called and he's left us alone.

"Come on, we're going for a drive." Cristiano tugs me to standing and pulls me along, while his two goons do the same with Adria and Calista. As we walk through the darkened restaurant, I wish that someone will notice what's going on, but all the patrons are deep in their own conversations. "And don't try anything because I'm already tempted to find out what Franco sees in you. Don't force my hand." The warning in his voice has me nodding.

When we arrive in the parking lot, there's a blacked-out SUV waiting, the engine running, and the door opens as we near it. Once inside, I'm wedged against a door I'm sure won't open if I try, but I know it would be stupid of me to attempt escape when they've got my cousin and best friend with sleek guns pointed at them.

Closing my eyes, I pray, beg, and plead with the gods, anyone who can hear, for Franco, Matteo, or Gio to find me, us. As the car pulls away, we sit in chilled silence.

THE RIDE SEEMS TO TAKE A LONG WHILE, AND AS MUCH AS I'M trying to gauge where we are by looking out the window, it's dark out. The only thing I can tell is that we're no longer on the highway. The back roads are dark or dimly lit, so nothing is clear from inside the vehicle.

Cristiano's body is pressed against mine as he holds me against him. My hands fist, and my nails dig into my palms to keep from crying, to just feel anything but this numbing fear that I'm about to get tortured or worse, killed.

I know Franco must be back at the house by now, and my phone hasn't buzzed once. Perhaps he was delayed in New York, but surely Gio would have noticed we're not back yet. Maybe he can't find me. *Does he have my number?* Yes. *Shit.* Too many thoughts race through my mind and as much as I want to, I can't still them. *Please, Franco, find us. Please.* I beg. I plead. And I pray.

I've never been religious. Never even been inside a church. But as the barrel of a gun rests against my ribs, I find religion in anything. In anyone. And I pray with all my heart and soul.

I've only just found real passion, real love. I've finally found myself and I can't lose it. I need to fight. I need to be strong. Glancing at my cousin and best friend, I can see them trembling, as I am. Fear. It's such a wicked emotion. It changes you. It can either strengthen you, or it can weaken you. When Calista's eyes meet mine, she offers a small, reassuring smile. One that tells me she's trying to be strong. We all are.

But strength doesn't come easy, you have to fight for it. You have to convince yourself you can do anything. Dad always used to tell me I was a strong little girl. I didn't cry much when I would get hurt. He once said I could be a queen if I set my mind to it. Now, thinking about it, I wonder if he meant ruling an organization like Franco's. It's the only answer I can come up with.

In my heart, I know Franco will find me. I am convinced he'll save me. As much as he wants to believe he's not a hero, nothing can change my mind knowing he is a good person. He's my knight in shining armor.

"*Siamo qui.*" A gruff tone comes from the driver's seat and the doors on either side of us open. I'm shoved out of the car and stumble onto the harsh gravel. The stones bite into my palms and I can't stop the tears that burn my eyes. A strong hand around my bicep has me whimpering as he tugs me to my feet.

"I see now why he's so enamored with you. Those precious sounds you make are intoxicating, Raina. Is that what you sound like when your cunt is filled with thick, hard cock?" His face is inches from mine as he hisses the words. The stench of whiskey is thick in his breath and I stifle the urge to retch.

"Let me go." The plea falls into the air between us and he laughs. It's a full, throaty sound as if I've just told him the funniest joke he's ever heard. Without answering, he tugs me toward the monstrosity that lies before us.

Even in the dark of the night sky, I can tell it's bigger

than any home I've ever been in, including the Moretti house. The double wooden doors that look like they've been carved from a tree trunk slide open and the light from inside blinds me momentarily.

Once inside, my eyes flit left to right, taking in the beauty of the house. A sweeping staircase fit for a queen with gilded railings on either side beckons, and as we head toward it, my heart leaps into my throat when a familiar man steps out from the shadows of a doorway.

His eyes meet mine. His smirk is cruel and evil, and my heart cracks. My world tips on its axis and the tears that threatened me since Cristiano first sat beside me finally tumble and my cheeks burn with the poisoned emotion that streaks down my face.

How could he do this to me? To Adria and Calista? Confusion swirls in my mind and I feel dizzy from the emotion that seems to choke me.

17

FRANCO

Storming into the office, with my body vibrating in rage, I feel him behind me. Gio was meant to watch her for two fucking days. Forty-eight hours and he couldn't even do that. "Look, I had to go sort out some shit. I couldn't take her to see what I do, what we do. You didn't want her involved in the business."

"So you're pinning this on me because I was trying to keep her safe?" Spinning on my heel, I meet his angry glare with one of my own. The air around us crackles with fury. It's dripping off him and I know it's my fault for doing this. I told her the truth about her father and mine, but I didn't tell her the reason I had brought her here. She didn't need to know, but I have a feeling she will find out soon enough.

When I found the document in my father's safe, I thought it was a joke. That he had set it there as a test of my loyalty, but when I dug into the background of little Raina Lombardi, I found out the truth. She wasn't just the daughter of my father's best friend, but she is also the heir to his fortune. The same fortune her brother is stealing from her.

When I found out the truth behind Andrea Lombardi, I

set a plan in motion to save her. To be her fucking knight in shining armor. And here I am, already failing. "Brother, we'll find them. We know where they are." Giovanni's right. We do know where they're being held. I just need to call in reinforcements and we'll take that fucker down. We'll rip him to shreds and slowly as I watch his life drain from his soulless green eyes, I'll smile. Because I'll be the victor.

"Get on the phone. I want everyone here. I'm done playing games with our *cugino,* I need him to pay." Cristiano has been the bane of my existence since we were children. The family we grew up in was filled with violence and secrets. There's no reason for us to be friendly, but his actions have taken a toll.

With that, we set to work. Tonight, I'll have more than a dozen of our *cosca,* or clan, in the house. We'll talk, plan, and we'll pull out all the weapons needed. This house has many layers, and like an onion, I will peel them back until I find the truth hidden below. Until I find my woman.

There's only one thing that matters right now and that's saving Raina. I wanted her to be free of this life. When Lucio left his wish for me to protect her, I vowed to get her out of the organization, out of danger. But she's been pulled into it, too deep, too far.

I gave her the job in my office and the contract to make sure it all looked legit. I didn't plan on confessing to murdering her father, but now I'm faced with more than just a woman I wanted to fuck. A woman I wanted to claim as my submissive, my slave for six months.

I'm deeper into the agreement than I expected to be and I've given more than I thought I would. I've lost my heart and given her the one thing I swore I'd never do again. My love.

The thought jolts me into action, pulling up my email program. I type out a request to Carlos Silva, my Brazilian supplier. He'll be able to deliver everything I need in the least amount of time. The man who's taken my woman and her cousin is a snake. He slithers in and hides in plain sight. To take him down, I need to be as downright devious as him.

Hitting send, I glance up when Matteo strolls into the room. "They've got all three girls," he informs me, tension rolling off him in waves, and I realize he cares for Adria. The dark-haired beauty has gotten under my brother's cold exterior, and I nod in understanding. He's never been one to talk about his feelings, and this is him being as open and honest about caring for her as he'll ever be.

"We'll get them back. I've just emailed Carlos and asked him for a shipment that needs to arrive tomorrow. The FBI will be notified as soon as it's in Russo's hands and we'll take a step back. Dad taught us how to win, and I'm not going to lose this fucking war."

He nods, slumping into the chair opposite my desk with his phone in hand.

"Teo."

He glances up, and I can see the concern etched on his face.

"Trust me."

"I do. She asked me if I'd ever want her exclusively. We'd been fucking for weeks now, and when she asked me that, I said no." His words are filled with regret. Agony for not saying the right thing. I feel the same. My last conversation with Rai, I told her about her father. I didn't divulge her brother's nasty secret, but I told her the only reason she was here was for me to look out for her. Which was a lie.

I wonder if she saw it on my face. Saw the love and affection I hold for her. My phone ringing drags me from my concerns and I see Russo's name on the screen. Sliding to answer, I put the phone to my ear. "What?"

"I guess you've heard," he responds with a smirk. I can hear it in his tone. "Your girlfriend is quite a tasty treat. No wonder you're so in love with her."

"I don't know what you're talking about. My girlfriend was murdered, or do you not remember slitting her throat?" I bite out, trying to steer the conversation away from the one woman who now holds my heart.

"Oh, come on, Isabelle loved to be shared. I remember how much she cried out when me and two of my men took her beautiful body and used it. Such an incredible sight." He growls in my ear, taunting me with knowledge of what they did to her. I've seen the medical reports. Fuck, I'd seen her corpse.

"Don't you dare fucking speak about—"

"Now, now, Franco. You don't want what happened to her to happen to this blond *bambolina*, do you?" He sneers the word for *little doll* in a thick, vile tone and I want to see how well he speaks with blood spurting from his throat once I slice it open.

"What do you want?" I hiss into the receiver.

"You leave the US, take your little pet with you. Go back to Sicily. I govern your American soil." That's ridiculous. I'll never let that happen. My father worked hard for what he built and I won't let some asshole take that away.

"And you can guarantee the girls aren't hurt?" My tone is steel, no emotion, no fear.

"They're safe... for now." His threat hangs between us like a lead weight. It's about to drop because when I walk in there, I'm going to make sure he pays for everything he's done.

"Give me forty-eight hours." My request has Matteo glaring at me in shock. He shakes his head, but I need to buy time for Carlos to get what I need here, and for us to round up the clan. There's no telling what Cristiano is planning, even though I know what he's capable of.

"Forty-eight and counting, mio amico." He chuckles.

"I'm no friend of yours, Russo. Do you agree to the time, because if you don't and something happens—"

"Relax, I'll give you your time, but not a minute later. Tick tock, Moretti."

And with that, he hangs up, leaving me more frustrated. "I should have asked to speak to the girls. Just to hear if they're okay."

"He wouldn't have allowed you the courtesy." Gio's voice from the doorway has both me and Matteo staring at him. "He's an asshole. He'll play this to the end."

I nod. He will. But he doesn't know I can play this game better than anyone.

"Let's make sure the cards swing in our favor then."

"FRANCO MORETTI, SO GOOD TO SEE YOU, MAN." I'M GREETED the same way by all the men who enter my home. They're my familia, my clan. The people I know will have my back when this shit goes down. We've gathered in the conference room, a large area with a table big enough to fit a dozen people. The rest all file in, and I'm at the head of the table.

"I must be honest, when I called on all of you, I didn't expect such a large showing." I settle in the chair, watching them as their eyes dart around the room. "There's something you all should know before I ask you to risk your lives walking into the Russo compound. He's made this personal." I steeple my fingers and take one look at each man before me. "He's kidnapped the woman I love." As the words fall from my mouth, I know I can't take them back.

And as much as I know I should, I don't want to. The first time admitting you love someone is the first step to putting your heart in their hands.

It's the step that you take, handing over something precious, entrusting them with it and hoping with all your fucking soul they don't break it. The difference between me and Raina is that she is the one that I know will heal my heart. She'll be the salve to my brokenness. Somehow, she's burrowed herself into my being, into the essence of who I am, and she's shone her light inside me.

When I opened my eyes this morning and rolled over in bed to find myself alone, I knew right then and there that she was mine. I needed to wake up to her. I spent two weeks hiding within myself, trying to stop the feelings I have for her, but there's nothing that can stop it.

"Franco, you know we're here for you no matter the circumstances. You've helped our families more times than we can count. For me this isn't even a question of *will we*. The answer will be when do we leave. Let's take this asshole down." His accent, although from the north of Italy, is still strong even after spending most of his life in America.

"I agree with Alessandro. There's no question. I'm in." As we go through each man's comments, they're all astounding me by standing behind me with this. Granted, it's part of the family, the Nostra, but for them to do this for a woman they've never met. This means more to me than I can ever explain.

"I've spoken to our contact in Brazil, Carlos Silva. He's agreed to help. A shipment of the finest narcotics will arrive in the country. We need a plan to get onto the Russo compound and plant it so that when the FBI are alerted, they'll find it. Once they do a background check on our friend, Cristiano Russo, they'll find all they need to put him away for a very long time."

"I have the blueprints of the mansion, the grounds, and the outbuildings. There are a number of places where we can gain entry." Gio sets the blueprints on the table, and as we pour over it, I take a step back and let my men take charge.

They've each got a role in the clan. They have specific talents. That's why they've been chosen. And they're all ruthless killers. Some of them with the bare hands, and some with weapons of choice. But we're all out for blood. It's how we've made it in, and it will be how we leave.

Our payment is done by the amount of bodies we pile up, not innocent bystanders, but scum like the Russos. All the men in this room know what he did. They knew my father. I grew up around most of them. So when I look around, it's not strangers getting together to avenge their friend, it's family.

"You okay, Franco?"

I turn to regard my younger brother and nod. "Yes, I'll be even better when we get our girls back." When I cast a longer glance at Matteo, I see the emotion in his eyes. He really does care for her. "You know, Adri is a beautiful girl."

He nods but doesn't respond.

"She's probably thinking about you, waiting for you to save her." I'm taunting him, but it's all in good fun, and when he turns to face me, there's a small smirk hidden behind his suave exterior.

"Don't pussyfoot around. Just say what you want to say, brother," he retorts.

"I know you want the girl. Don't hold back. You never know when it will be your last chance to tell her how you feel." We stare at each other for a long while and he nods. He knows I'm right. In our life, in the lifestyle we follow, tomorrow is never promised. And I know that's true for most people, but with threats that come from left, right, and center, we never know when our last breath will be.

"Take your own advice, old man." He pats me on the shoulder, and the playfulness I know my little brother to have is there, hidden underneath the tension of the situation we're in.

18

RAINA

"Why are you doing this? Where is he?"

The man who took me, the man who killed Franco's father, bores his gaze into me and it's as if he's choking me.

"You're a pretty girl. I can see why Franco keeps you around. Is your cunt as sweet as your pretty blue eyes?" He smirks. "I'm not a bad man, *carina*." He stalks around me. His gaze trails from my face to my feet. I'm bound to the seat with my feet tied with thick ropes to the legs of the chair. He stops before me, leaning in with his hands on either armrest. "You see, *bella,* men like us... we prefer, decadence. And it seems Franco and I have the same taste."

Anger heats my blood. I'm not scared of him anymore. I want to spit in his face, but I don't want to force him to do something stupid. They've not hurt us and if I can buy some time, I know that Franco won't let me die. He will save us. I just don't know how.

"I'd like to taste what Franco finds so alluring about you." He rises, snaps his fingers, and two men enter the room. They untie me and lift me by my upper arms. Both have a tight grip and there's no chance I can even get away, should I want to try. "Take her to my suite. Make sure she's"—he smirks as he regards me—"comfortable." With that, I'm dragged out of the room and down a long hallway.

I don't know where Adria and Calista are. I haven't seen them since we arrived and got separated. Glancing around, I take in the hallway. The artwork on the walls reminds me of a museum. It's dimly lit, but the opulence gives away the wealth that lies within these walls.

My two captors stalk toward a set of double doors. And as much as I'd like to try to fight them, I know it will be pointless. They're both easily six feet tall and built like brick walls. There's no way I can do anything to them that they'll even notice.

They drag me into a suite that could possibly fit into the apartment I share with my cousin. Once I'm bound to yet another chair, they leave and I'm left to my thoughts. Memories of Franco, of what we've done, how he's made me feel, all of it hits me and I'm left breathless. Sadness envelops me. It cocoons me in the surety that I'm alone here. Even though I know Cali and Adi are somewhere in this mansion, without the man who's stolen my heart, I am alone.

Suddenly, the door flies open and I meet the luminous green eyes of Cristiano Russo. "You look beautiful in my bedroom. I was hoping they'd bound you to my bed. I'm sure seeing you on those black satin sheets would have been my ultimate fantasy come true." He smirks, stalking toward me. My body reacts, and a shudder wracks through me.

"Why are you doing this?"

"You don't know? Did Daddy not tell you how he tried to steal my fortune?" he questions hotly. The anger in his gaze tells me I don't know a thing about my father. "Oh, *bella,* so innocent and sweet. You were my first choice in payment. I'm guessing your boyfriend didn't tell you?" When my gaze darts to him in shock and surprise, he chuckles darkly. "Well, it seems Franco doesn't trust you enough to tell you the whole truth."

Confusion swirls, anger heats my blood, and my stomach rolls with a sick feeling that I can't squash down. He turns to me then. Stalking toward me, he leans in and trails my cheek with his lips. His tongue darts out and flicks over my mouth.

"*Mio caro*, you do taste like heaven. You see, *bella,* your father tried to steal my money. And then your boyfriend just walked in and took it all for himself. This is why I'm taking what matters most to him."

"I don't matter to him." My retort is met with a heated glare.

"You fucking matter. He's in love with you," he bites back, his hand slamming against my cheek. The chair flings over and I find myself on the floor. The metallic taste of blood in my mouth has me retching. "After all he's taken from me, he wants more, every fucking time." He growls and his foot finds my ribs, slamming the breath from my lungs, and tears burn my eyes.

The cough and splutter that falls from my lips is enough fuel to earn me one more shove. Then his fists are in my hair, tugging me up. Pulling a blade from his holster, he slices the ropes that bind my legs but leaves my hands tied. He tugs me back, and the sleek silver pops the buttons on the blouse I was wearing and when it falls open I'm met with a heated stare.

"No wonder Franco is so invested in you. Look at those beautiful tits." He reaches out, his index finger running along my jaw, down my collarbone, and over my chest and cleavage. "I bet those beautiful rosy nipples taste as sweet as your skin. And does your cunt taste like strawberries, *bella*?"

"Fuck you." My retort shocks me and him. He rears back. Green eyes pin me with pure venom. I've never seen rage so undiluted before.

"I wish you would. You mistake me for a bad man, Raina. But I don't take what doesn't belong to me. I also don't force a woman to accept my dick unless she's begging for it."

"I'll never beg."

That has him laughing, a full, throaty chuckle. "Oh, I knew you'd say that. Even if my dick never touches your sweet lips, I'll know that one day you'll beg me. It might not be today, and it might not be in the next month or two, but there will come a time when you'll ask for my lenience, for mercy. Remember this life you've chosen to walk along isn't easy. There isn't good or bad. We're all one and the same."

He's right. Franco isn't good, and he isn't bad. Neither am I. Lifting my gaze, I meet Cristiano's and nod. I agree. A smile cracks his handsome face and I can't help but wonder what pain he suffered to be so volatile. He releases his hold on me and I consider running but find myself intrigued by this man.

"You know, sometimes my father used to tell me why people are evil."

He stops and regards me. As if waiting for a confession he's waited for his whole life.

"He said people are only angry at life for something they've been through. They hurt others to make themselves feel better for the pain they've endured." Our gazes are locked in a standoff and then I see it. My words have affected him and in the depths of green, a flame so slight flickers. I regard the man I first saw as evil, but now that I look at him, and I mean really look at him, I see the pain in his eyes.

"Men are weak when they love. That is why I don't allow such trivial emotions into my life. Love. It's a sickness. It makes stronger men weak. It makes kings fall. And it makes warriors lose in battle," he grunts out, but with every word, I can feel the lies dripping off them.

"And you've lost a war before? Have you fallen?" I question. I'm completely out of my element. He's the bad guy, but when he regards me, there's no malice. Only sadness. Breath-stealing sorrow.

"Ah, *bella,* such sweetness and innocence. Yes, I did love. A long time ago."

His gaze drops from mine and I feel it then.

The pain. The uncertainty. The heartbreak.

"You're quite the siren, aren't you, Raina?" he questions, lifting his green-eyed gaze to mine again. I don't respond, but I take in his distress. I drink it like a cocktail. A mixture of fear, love, anger, lust, and desire. It's an intoxicating blend of everything I feel for Franco.

"Who was she?" I answer his question with one of my own. He regards me for a long while. Too long before he steps back and turns his attention to the windows before us.

"A woman I could never have," he tells me, but his eyes never meet mine. The surrounding air is heavy with contemplative emotion. He's been hurt before. Had his heart broken. Sometimes monsters love as well. I wish I could go to him. But my fear holds me back.

"Would you let me loose?" I question. When he spins on his heel, he immediately falls at my feet and grips the blade from his holster, slicing the ropes that hold my wrists. Without thinking and my hands free, I reach for his face.

My hand tentatively caresses his jaw, which has a light dusting of stubble.

"I can see why he loves you. Your touch, it's...." Lifting those deep green pools, he stares at me for so long I'm sure he's forgotten what he wanted to tell me. "You're like a drug," he murmurs.

Smiling wryly, I regard him. "That's what..." my words falter when he stares at me.

"Franco?" he questions and I nod. "You know, we grew up together. He was like a brother to me. For years. When I chose the wrong side, I lost him along with the only woman I ever loved because she chose my best friend." He chuckles wryly.

"The woman you loved, she chose Franco?" My brows furrow in confusion and my heart leaps into my throat with the new knowledge of the man I love with another.

He nods with a sad smile, but as soon as it arrived, it's gone. "Life moves on. I did." He pushes up and turns to the window once more. I risk a glance at my wrists. They're marked lightly with the pattern of the rope. "I'm sorry I have to do this, Raina. I've always done bad things. I've always chosen the wrong side. After I lost everything, I became..."

"Angry?" Dragging my gaze to him, I watch the suit jacket crinkle with his movements. He places both hands flat on the windowpane and drops his head. Pushing off the chair, I take a few steps toward him. The knife is still in his hand and my heart thuds in my chest.

As soon as I reach him, he spins on his heel, grabbing me by the throat and pinning me between his solid torso and the wall. His body heat warms me and his breath fans over my face. "I became a monster. I hurt people. I watch them die and you know what, Raina?"

I shake my head as his grip around my neck gets tighter.

"I love it. It makes me hard. It's like sex. Feral, animalistic, and raw."

My body shudders beneath his. My throat works to swallow and he eases his grip. Our heated gazes are locked on each other. I can feel his rigid erection pressing against my thigh and when my eyes fall to his lips, they curve into a smirk, so devilish it's almost sinful.

"You see, *bella,* I can make you ache. I can make you crave it. And you know why?" He leans in further, his lips nipping at the lobe of my ear. "Because you like the dark, you like it rough. Your pupils are dilated, and your pussy, that sweet little cunt, it's hot and wet for me right now. Isn't it?"

As much as I want to deny it, as much as I want to shake my head and disagree, I can't. Because I am needy, but not for him. The way he's pinned me, the scent of his spicy cologne, they all remind me of Franco. "I'm only turned on because you remind me of him." Once the words fall from my lips, I find myself being flung onto the bed. Before I have time to find my bearings, he's on top of me. His body pressing me into the mattress as he bucks his hips into my ass, grinding his cock against me.

19

FRANCO

The grounds are dimly lit. Getting onto his property wasn't an easy feat and as I walk up to the basement door, I shudder to think what's happening inside. With Matteo's computer wizardry, he managed to override the alarm system.

The ten men, armed with guns, took out the outer perimeter of guards Russo had along the walls. Getting in wasn't challenging. The problematic part is coming up. Entering the house will be interesting because I know the layout. We've all seen the blueprints, but as I push the door of the pantry open, I'm met with silence.

I'm not sure where he's holding the girls, but with the amount of men I have behind me, we'll find them quickly. Allowing six of the ten armed killers in before me, I keep my Glock tight in my hand. There's a round of metal in here that I'm dying to unload into Cristiano's skull.

Edging our way in, I watch as Gio and Lorenzo take down two guards. The doors to the living area slide open and we're all bathed in dim light. For a man this dangerous, his clan isn't as sharp as I thought they'd be. In no time, I'm climbing the stairs and heading toward what I'm guessing are the bedrooms.

Muffled sounds come from each door and with a show of my hand, I point in the direction of the entrances to whatever atrocities are happening behind them. I know where I'm headed. The master suite. The only place I know he would have taken her.

It's been years. Cristiano and I grew up together.

Best fucking friends.

Until a woman came between us.

He blamed me. She chose me.

I hated her.

It was a fate worse than death. I dated her for a short while before I finally admitted defeat. I never loved her the way she wanted, the way he did. When I moved on with my life and found Isabella, I fell hard and fast. She was my first slave. The first woman I owned. With her, I saw forever. But my best friend had already made up his mind. He'd had it out for me for years after the woman he loved chose me. He left Isabella in a pool of crimson on his bedroom floor.

And now that I've finally allowed love back into my life, my heart, finally moved on, he's attempting to take it away.

Nothing could prepare me for feeling this anguish. The throb inside my chest when I think of her being hurt. Raina Lombardi has slowly embedded her innocence inside me. She's given me everything I didn't know I wanted.

But with that, she's also taken my darkness, she's fed the beast, and somehow flourished with it. She dances with the blackened soul I hold, as if she craves it. When I reach the end of the long hallway, the double doors tell me I've arrived. My future lies on the other side of those doors.

Gripping the knob with my free hand, I lift the gun and shove open the door to find a sight that boils my blood. Rage turns my vision red and I command as I enter, "Get the fuck off my woman." My voice booms through the bedroom and both Raina and Cristiano still. His glare pins me to the spot and his mouth lifts into a smirk.

"Franco, so good to see you. I can tell why you're so enamored with this beauty," he murmurs as he gets up off my girl. Righting his jacket, he stalks toward me, stepping in front of the barrel as if he's not afraid to die.

"Get on your fucking knees, now."

With a smirk, confident and sure, he drops to his knees.

"Rai, are you okay?" I call to her as I step around him. Her curves find themselves molded to my body and her face is buried in the crook of my arm.

"Franco, the other girls," she murmurs.

"They'll be okay. I've brought a few friends."

Cristiano chuckles darkly from the floor, and I rear back my gun and get him on the side of the head. His body slumps forward, out cold. With him debilitated, I have a moment to regard my girl. Her body is shaking and her blouse hangs open.

"Did he…"

I can't bring myself to say the words. She shakes her head quickly, but when those blue eyes meet mine, there's something else there. "He was… he just spoke to me." Dragging her gaze to his unconscious body, she looks at him with something akin to affection. Jealousy roars in my ears and I reach for her chin, lifting it so her eyes are on me.

"What the fuck did he tell you?" The words are hoarse, rough with emotion that seems to be dragging me under. I'm tempted to put a bullet in his skull right now. But she reaches for my gun and I willingly allow her to take it.

"He told me about your friendship, and he made me realize something." Her voice drops an octave lower as she leans up on her tiptoes. Her lips at my ear when she finally says it. The words that knock the wind from my lungs. "I love you, Franco."

Just then, before I can respond, the doors fly open and three of my men stop dead in their tracks. "Take him away," I order and they nod, but not before offering Raina a small smile. Turning to regard her, I cup her face in my hands and plant a soft kiss to her lips. It's not hungry, it's not animalistic, it's passionate. It tells her what I can't voice. I pour my love for her into the kiss. Allowing her to breathe it in. To taste it. To consume it.

"Franco." Gio's voice from behind me forces me to break the kiss. When I meet his eyes, there's horror painted on his expression.

"What happened?" My tone is ice when I say the name with fear racing through my veins. "Cali—"

He shakes his head. "Calista is a bit banged up, but she's okay. It's..." His voice drops as he flits a quick glance at Rai, then back at me. "It's Adria. She's hurt."

***

"Baby."

Rai stirs and blinks away the sleep from her eyes. She's exhausted, but she's refused to leave the hospital bed. When we found out her best friend had been hurt so badly, she couldn't move. Needless to say my brother was beside himself. I'd never seen Matteo so fucked up before.

When we rushed her to the hospital, I lost two men in the process when their car was wrecked. I don't fucking know what happened, but Cristiano managed to shoot one and overpower the other. The fucker escaped, but I've got a search going for him. When I find that asshole, he'll pay. This time, it will be with his life.

He was right. I've never killed if it wasn't warranted.

There was information I needed from him. That's why I didn't put a bullet in him. Also, I wanted to make sure Raina was safe. I should have shot the fucker when I saw him lying on top of her.

Handing her the coffee, I settle into the chair beside hers and watch the machines beep. The respirator lifts and drops with each breath.

Matteo's asleep in the corner. He's not left the room. It's been three days and my brother hasn't moved. The only time he's gotten up is to shower and take a piss. And even then, it's in the en suite bathroom. There are dark circles under his eyes. He looks like shit, to be honest.

Luckily, we can afford the best care. So the hospital has set up a private room, as well as giving us all hour access. Although, I think if they told him to leave, he'd kick up such a huge fuss, they'd give in anyway.

Leaning in, I whisper, "I think you need a break. Come with me." Teary blue pools dart to me and she nods with a small smile.

I want to take her out of here, for fresh air, just to calm her down. Lacing my fingers with hers, I tug her into me as we quietly shut the door. There's a stairwell that leads to the roof and I guide her that way. With each clinking step, I can feel the tension leaving her body.

Pushing the door open, I allow her to step out first. The sun is shining brightly and the air is thick with summer heat. From up here, you can see for miles. Los Angeles has always been one of my favorite places. The people, the weather, the wine—although I do prefer the Italian blends —it has a certain charm to it.

"I'm worried about her, Franco. She's broken. She's so fucking broken." Her words fall on a raspy whisper and I pull her into my embrace. When she breaks down, it feels as if my heart is being ripped from my chest. I wish I could make things better, but I can't. I wish I could fix Adria's body, but I can't.

Those fuckers did a number on her. Luckily, Calista wasn't harmed, besides a few cuts and scrapes. And thank God Raina wasn't hurt. "Tell me, *bella*." She shudders at the word and I step back to regard her. "Did he hurt you?"

She's quiet for a while as if she's contemplating what to tell me. However, at this point, I need the truth. I need the anger to fuel me so when I find that asshole, I'll not think twice.

"He hit me, once. I was tied to a chair. When it fell, he kicked me a couple of times." Her confession rakes through me. Slicing my heart, flaying it, and allowing it to pour emotion from my chest. The need to kill and maim runs rife through my veins.

"I'll find him, baby. I'll find him and I'll fucking kill him." I vow. There'll be blood on my hands. There's no doubt about that, but I will avenge everything she and the other two girls have been through.

"Franco, there's one more thing," she murmurs. Lifting her eyes, she looks at the sky, blinks, and then pins me with a questioning stare. "When we arrived at the house. He was taking me to the room where I was tied up and…"

"What, Rai? You need to tell me."

"My brother was there. I saw Andrea walking out of one of the rooms with two other men."

I promised I'd never tell her. I vowed that the secret would stay with me to my death, but I can't keep it anymore. I need to be honest. I need to explain to the woman I love that her brother isn't hers by blood. Instead, he's a snake. An undercover mole for the Russos.

"*Mio caro.*" Reaching for her face, I cup her cheek in one hand, my thumb teasing circles over the smooth, rosy skin. "Andrea is not your brother."

Her brows furrow and she attempts shaking her head.

"He's... fuck, I didn't want you to find out like this." Dropping my hand, I turn away from her, not wanting to see the pain in her eyes.

She's been through so much already and now I'm only going to pile on more shit. Her hand on my shoulder has me turning to regard her. "Tell me. I can handle it."

"Andrea is a Russo. He's Cristiano's cousin."

Shock paints her expression. I knew it would. I wait for the anger, but it doesn't come. I thought she'd be angry that I didn't tell her. Actually, I wanted her to be angry because I should have been honest. But as she regards me, I don't see it.

"I never knew. I mean... He's always been different, more volatile. Why didn't my parents ever tell me?"

I shrug. Honestly, I don't know the reason her parents even took him in as their own. He's a fucking bastard child. One that I plan on getting rid of as soon as we find the fucker. Her father worked both sides of the coin. Most of the men who get killed do. They get greedy, only seeing the dollar signs, and they end up paying with their lives. The Nostra aren't easy people to deal with. You fuck us over then you find yourself six feet under.

"Look, *bella,* there are a lot of unexplained stories that float around with these people. I wish I had more answers for you, but so far, that's all I know. It's something we're working on uncovering, but I can't tell you more." I pull her in for a cuddle. I'm not the type of man who enjoys this sort of thing, but having her body mold to mine is an exquisite thing.

"Franco, take me to the dark room."

"With pleasure."

20

RAINA

The lights are dim. I asked for this. I'm not sure what he's about to do, but I can only imagine it's going to have me soaring with pleasure.

"Get into position."

Before I have time to think, my body obeys. Dropping to my knees, I wait for his command.

I hear his footfalls on the wooden floor. They move around the room and then I feel the heat of him behind me.

"Are you ready to experience me, Rai, with no limits?"

"Yes, Sir," I murmur.

"Good girl," he whispers on a smile. "I want you to stand, strip, and wait with your feet shoulder-width apart. I want your hands behind your back and your eyes closed."

Nodding, I start my show for him. I can feel him watching and my body turns molten.

I fold my clothes and place them in the corner of the room. Once my panties and bra are lying atop the rest of my clothes, I pad barefoot back to the spot he's asked me to stay in. Standing, I face the window and grip my hands behind my back. My legs are spread just the way he likes and my eyes flutter closed.

"You're beautiful, *bella*." His voice comes from behind me and I can't help reveling in his words. "I'm going to do something to you tonight that's going to push you outside of your comfort zone. It's going to make you scream, cry, and I'm going to fuck you so hard, I'll be the only man you'll ever need. If you feel it's too much, you have your safe word. Do you remember it?"

"Yes, Sir."

"Good girl."

With those two words, he grips my wrists and walks me over to the table he fucked me on, which sits at the window. He positions me on the cool wood. I'm kneeling comfortably, but a second later, my body is bent at the waist and I find my wrists at my ankles. A soft leather cuff circles my left wrist and clicks into place. He does the same with my right limbs. I'm now bound, locked in place with my most intimate areas bared to him.

"So fucking beautiful," he murmurs in awe. With a featherlight touch, he strokes my thighs, sending jolts of pleasure through me. His big hands grip my ass, squeezing it hard, making me whimper out loud. "No noise, *bella,*" he orders in a gruff but raspy tone.

It's silent for a long moment and my ears prickle with the sound of a soft whoosh. A whip.

"Ready?"

"Yes, Sir," I respond, but my body trembles, not from fear but anticipation. But the sting doesn't come and I'm confused. Then I feel it. The cool liquid I can only guess is lube being trickled on my puckered entrance. "Oh God!" The words are out before I can stop them and I'm awarded with a harsh swat of his hand. Biting my lip to keep from screaming out, I shut my eyes and breathe through my nose.

He starts teasing my ass with an index finger, slowly

and gently, but it has my body prickling and sizzling. I feel a second finger then. It enters me and he continues his ministrations, scissoring me open. Readying me.

Silence sits heavy around and I'm tempted to beg. Or plead. But I know it will earn me punishment. Once I'm squirming and pushing back against his fingers, he pulls them from me. A second later, cool metal meets the forbidden entrance. A butt plug. He works it in, as if he's scared of hurting me, and as soon as it pops past the tight ring of muscle, he growls.

"That's going to be my cock soon, Raina."

The leather whip whooshes and then the bite comes. It's a cat o' nine tails and each leather strap hits various parts of my thighs, ass, and pussy. Keeping silent is becoming difficult, but I bite down on my lip. Another swat and another. Every inch of my body is alight. Needy. My pussy is soaked, drenched with need for him to take me. But he continues his torture. In my head, I count twelve, but I can't be certain because when he finally drops the whip, I'm floating above myself.

A buzzing sound startles me, but his hands massage my ass that's hot from the lashes. "So fucking beautiful with my mark on your creamy skin. And your cunt, it's wet. So fucking wet. But if you come, I'll punish you. Do you hear me?" he warns.

"Y-ye-yes, S-sir..." I hiss through clenched teeth.

As soon as the words leave my lips, I'm impaled by a thick plastic dildo. That's all it can be because it's cold. Cool. Not a cock. Not Franco. My head spins out of control from the pleasure and pain. He rains down swat after swat on my red ass while I'm filled beyond anything I've ever experienced. "I need your ass, Rai," he growls.

I'm still full when he tugs the butt plug and before I have time to miss the feeling, Franco drives into my ass so deep I can't be quiet anymore. I cry out so loudly, I'm beyond pain, I'm in subspace. I've heard of it, but never knew it existed. I thought it wasn't real.

"Good girl. Feel me. Ground yourself to me, *bella*," he murmurs but doesn't stop his assault on my ass. My pussy clenches around the dildo and my ass squeezes his cock. I know this because he tells me. He spanks me. He drives into me. He claims me. He fucks me. He owns me.

My body is boneless; my mind is soaring above us. Watching two people connect and fuck like animals, but this is what I need. What my body craves.

Suddenly, he grips my hips and bites out, "I'm going to fill your little ass, baby." With each word, he drives in and out, in and out. "I'm going to mark every inch of your beautiful skin." His fingers dig painfully into my hips and I know he's marking every inch of my skin. "You are mine, Rai, all fucking mine."

He grunts. I nod.

He plunges. I cry out.

"Come for me, *bella*," he roars and as his body locks, mine shudders. My eyes roll back in my head. I can't get a grip on anything. My throat hurts. Burns from screaming. Tears stream down my face. And I splinter. I shatter. And he's there to hold me as warm jets of his release fill me.

THE PARTY DOWNSTAIRS IS IN FULL FORCE, WITH THE THUMP OF the bass vibrating through the walls, through me. A harsh swat on my ass silences me. That's when I hear the soft sounds of his slacks and boxers being pushed down. I hear the foil being torn by sharp teeth. And then I'm filled. A thick cock inside my tight body and his fingers on my hips.

Lucio is finally claiming what is his. And I'm lost in the bliss of his touch, his lips. He kisses my neck, and bites down gently. I've dreamed of this for so long, and now it's happening.

"Is this what you wanted, Raina?" His smooth voice is a whisper, a gentle rasp. My head spins as the pain slowly subsides. Even though it still hurts having him inside me, I welcome the pain. He waited till I was eighteen.

My dirty secret.

My dark desire.

He is mine for in this moment. There is nothing else that matters right now. He is mine. And I am his. I always have been. He just took longer to realize it.

"Yes, Lucio." My murmur is tinged with desire, filled with guilt, but my body, the traitorous bitch, is needy. Wet for the bad man who hides in the shadows before me.

"You're going to be an asset to me. You, little principessa." He groans while his hands grip my ass. His voice is huskier, deeper than usual.

"Why me?"

Without answering, he tugs my head back, allowing a whimper to fall from my lips. "Because your tight little eighteen-year-old cunt is delicious. And, when Moretti comes for you, I'll know deep down I've had you first." I'm confused. I've never met this person he mentioned.

"What—"

"I'll fuck you every day if I have to. So when he slides inside you, and no doubt he will, you'll have had me first," he bites out as I fist the sheets, taking his brutal attack.

I moan and whimper. His drives press me into the mattress. "I don't—"

"Raina..."

"Raina..."

"RAINA!"

Jolting upright, I find dark eyes piercing me.

Franco. Shit.

"What the fuck were you dreaming about?" He needs to know. I have to tell him. I can't hold secrets like this anymore. It's going to destroy me.

"I have to tell you something. You're not going to like it."

He watches me, narrowing his eyes. Taking me in with that shrewd stare.

"I fell into my need for danger when I was fifteen. Lucio bombarded my life, and he made me *feel*. I begged him for more, but he never would touch me. He treated me as an equal though. He would talk about work, things I shouldn't know about."

Franco regards me with a curious stare. As the dream still grips me, I can't help shivering at the memory of my stupidity.

"Lucio was just out of reach, all those years. Even as we grew closer, I knew he would never be able to offer me what I so craved. I wanted him. But his life was this world, the organization. And I..." My words taper off and I fidget with the sheet. My body is still tingling with the memory of *him*. "After turning eighteen, I needed to be free of the confines of my father's rules, so I snuck out of the house to go to a party. Lucio messaged me that night, and told me he would be there to see me."

"Rai—"

"He gave me orders, like he always did. Go to the bedroom and wait. When he entered, he didn't put on the light, but I felt him. I was convinced it was him. I was deliriously happy; I didn't second guess it because he was finally going to claim me."

Anger rolls over the man before me as his fists clench.

Jealousy. Rage. All the emotions I'd expected sit heavily between us.

"I'm sorry I didn't tell you." My voice is breaking with every word I utter.

"It's Cristiano, isn't it?"

I can't say the words. For a long, heavy silent moment, I breathe deeply. "I had known Lucio for such a long time, it was what I wanted. But then... but when I saw Cristiano, something struck me." My voice is raspy as I try to respond. "Lucio and I were together for a while until his death, but that night was different. Now when I recall it, I realize how strange it was. There was one time he said something I didn't understand."

"Rai, you need to tell me," Franco urges, and I know I have to be honest.

"He... He said that you would one day come for me, and you'll know that he had me first." A sob falls from my lips, and he places a finger under my chin, lifting my head up. My eyes meet his, my brows furrow in confusion.

"Lucio and Cristiano were brothers," Franco whispers slowly as the realization dawns on him. Then, as if a cloud slowly descends over him, he says, "I want you in the playroom. On your knees. Naked. Waiting." That's all he says before walking out and leaving me a nervous wreck. Pushing off the bed, I pad over to the door and make my way to the room where he's about to punish me with pain and pleasure.

The door is cracked, and I notice the glowing light of candles. Stepping inside, I find it empty. I pull off the tank top I'm wearing and push down the panties, placing them in the corner as I've been trained. The room is warm, but there's tension radiating from me, which causes me to shiver involuntarily.

I drop to my knees as instructed with my head down

and my palms up. The door creaks and I feel him. His energy overwhelms me.

"Good girl. You're so pretty on your knees," he murmurs. When he steps into my line of sight, the shiny black shoes are the only thing I see. A hiss of a zipper sends a tingle of awareness through me. "Today, you're going to take me. You're going to feel me everywhere, *bella*," he affirms as he shuffles his slacks down what I know are thick, muscled thighs.

I hear more material shifting and I realize his briefs are now lowered as well.

"Eyes up."

I obey. A hard, angry erection juts out toward me. My mouth waters to taste him. To please him.

"Swallow my dick, little one."

And I do. My lips move slowly over the crown, taking him into the warmth between my lips. His head falls back the deeper I suck him. When the tip hits the back of my throat, I choke, but I know he likes the sound, so I do it again and again.

His hands grip my long blond strands and he fists them painfully. The sting causes me to moan, which in turn vibrates my throat around his shaft.

"Fuck." His growl is feral. He pulls out and slams back in. It's torture. It's brutal. It's him. He fucks my face, my mouth, my throat. Spit drips from my chin onto my breasts, but he doesn't relent. Just as his body locks, he pulls out and shoots his hot seed on my lips, cheeks, and chest. "You're marked, Raina. You're mine."

Without another word, he pulls me to stand and walks me over to a leather bench. Positioning me on my back, he lays me down and proceeds to tie my wrists to metal cuffs. Then my legs are spread wide with a thick metal bar, which he locks in place, making me bend at the waist. I'm open.

Lewdly so. But the fire in his gaze turns me molten. It burns me from the inside out.

"Now I'm going to punish you for not telling me sooner. And I'm going to fuck any memory of that asshole from your mind."

He reaches for a leather riding crop. Taking his time, he gently, lightly trails a path over my thighs, ass, and clit, which has my hips jerking wildly. He moves over to my nipples, taunting them the same way. And then it starts. He lifts the leather and swats one peaked bud, then the other. Again and again. The pain, the pleasure, everything sears my nerves and shoots through my veins.

By the time he stops, I've lost count. My breasts are red, tingly, and I'm aching for more. I watch as he positions himself at my spread legs. Lifting the crop, he brings it down on my clit. "Fuck!" My cry is loud. I've never felt anything like it.

"Close your eyes, breathe, and do not make a noise," he orders and I can't help whimpering. He continues his assault on my pussy, my clit, and I'm biting down so hard on my lip I break skin. "Your cunt"—whack—"is mine." Whack. "Your ass"—whack—"is mine."

I can't speak. I can't think. I'm trembling. Needy. My orgasm has my body taut, painfully so, and all I need is his command, but it doesn't come. Instead, he drops the crop, grips his steel shaft, and slaps my clit with the crown. My body convulses, needing release.

Without warning, he plunges into my pussy so deep and so brutally, I don't doubt he's fucked every memory I've ever had, sexual or non, out of my mind. My brain short-circuits when he plunges in and out of me.

He pulls out, and I know what's coming. The warmth of my arousal drips down the crack of my ass and then he's there. Filling me with his fingers in my pussy. His cock violating me beautifully. His fingers drawing the pleasure from my heart and soul.

"I'm yours. You're mine." He continues thrusting as he grunts the words. And then he does it. He bites out two words as he pinches my clit. "Marry me." It's not the two I expected, but they detonate me and I splinter below him.

EPILOGUE
RAINA

Three months later

To learn the brother who you thought you knew was nothing more than a stranger in disguise causes you to re-evaluate connections. Knowing Andrea related to the man who almost raped you and would've killed you is another reason I have forced myself to come to terms with my past. Therapy helps. Talking about the worries that plague me about what I went through has given me a new outlook.

Don't bottle-up feelings.

I was never close to Andrea. We didn't always see eye to eye, so when Franco told me the truth, I wasn't hurt. Shocked, yes. Angry, definitely.

Hitting send on an email to confirm the payment of mine and Cali's inheritance into our designated bank accounts, I sit back and glance around the office. My six-month contract with the Morettis has ended, but I'm not leaving. Now I have a new contract, one as Franco's fiancée. But what else am I to this man? Submissive? Sex slave? I giggle at the thought.

While I finish my degree, I'll still work in the office, help with the daily running of what they do. Shipments, orders, emailing the suppliers and whatever else comes my way, but I'm now part of the family. I've been introduced as his partner. We're not married, yet, but I feel as if I've been accepted.

When the door swings open, Gio saunters in with his signature smoke hanging from his full lips. "Ciao, bella." He smirks. His thick accent and deep baritone sound more pronounced. He's just arrived back from Italy.

"Gio, please tell me how Adi is doing?" I haven't heard from her in a week. Although Matteo has texted once to let me know they'd arrived.

"She's a strong girl. She'll be fine. Time will heal and my brother will be there to care for her."

I nod. He's right. Matteo has been incredible with her. Even though she's pushed him away more times than I could count in the last few weeks, he's never strayed. He's stood by her, pushed her to accept that his support, his affection, isn't going anywhere. After her childhood, I'm glad she's found a man who isn't about to up and leave the moment things get tough.

"I've got that meeting with Carlos set up for a week from Friday. He wants to see you and Franco," I inform him. The smoke rings that filter from his mouth float into the air and his dark eyes pin me with an amused expression. "What?"

"You're quite a little firecracker, Raina." He smirks. "I'm happy for you and Franco. He needs someone who can kick his ass every now and then."

"Get out of my fucking office with your cigarette." The amused, yet commanding tone of the man in question startles us both and I watch as Gio holds up his hands in surrender. He rises to his full six-foot and stalks over to the balcony door. As Franco enters the office, I see the little blonde behind him.

"Cali!"

She squeals and rushes toward me. My cousin has been traveling. Her new modeling contract has kept her busy, which is good, considering everything that's happened over the last two months. She did a few shoots over the years, but when a client called her and asked her to fly to Europe, she jumped at the chance.

"Cali, how was Paris?"

"The food was amazing. The city itself is paradise. I loved it. Even though I was on set for most of it, the few snippets of time off were incredible." She gushes as Giovanni circles her waist.

"There's my beauty." He nuzzles her hair and another fit of giggles falls from her lips. "I missed you," he growls into her neck.

"Get a room, you two." Franco's chuckle comes from his desk, and I glance at him. Finding my handsome man with a wicked smirk on his full lips.

"Yeah, yeah, brother. We're leaving. Come on, baby. I want to show you how much I missed you." He tugs my cousin as she gives me a wave and blows a kiss in my direction before they exit and shut the door behind them.

"Come here, Rai. I want to show you how much I missed you." The raspy tone of his voice is enough to send a shudder through me. Rounding my desk, I make my way over to his and perch on the smooth mahogany top. "Mmm, I think you need to hike up that skirt, let me see those pretty panties you have hidden." His hooded gaze tells me I'm in for something decadent and naughty.

Without a second thought, I pull my pencil skirt up to my thighs and revel in the growl I'm met with when he sees the white satin material that hugs my now quivering entrance.

"Spread your legs, *bella*."

I obey. His big hands come down on my thighs and he pushes them wide. Obscenely so. Running his nose along my left inner thigh, he groans when he reaches my panty-clad pussy. He mimics the action on my right thigh and runs his nose along my panties. "You smell like a mid-morning snack, sweetheart," he rumbles.

His index finger teases the material until it's soaked with my arousal. Then he flattens his tongue and licks his way from my ass to my clit. "God, Franco." It's all he needs to hear. The panties get pushed to the side, and his mouth latches on to my glistening core. His tongue darts into my opening, and he devours me.

Just then, the phone in the office rings loudly, echoing through the lust that's swirling around us. "Answer the phone," he growls while feasting on my body. With a shaky hand, I reach for the phone and try to push him away, but he doesn't relent. "I'm not stopping. You'll need to find your center and not let them know what I'm doing." His words cause me to still in shock. "Do it. That's an order."

Knowing I can't refuse him, I lift the receiver and bring it to my ear. "Moretti residence. How can I help you?" My voice is meek at best, and as the caller responds, Franco goes back to licking me, nipping at the lips of my pussy, and slowly, gently, he sinks a finger into me.

Carlos tells me he'll be late for the meeting. "Okay, I'll, uh..."

"Carino, are you okay?" His baritone is filled with concern, and I know I need to find the words to assure him I'm fine.

"Yes, I'm... it's... busy here." Fingers sink deeper,

plunging in and out. When he crooks both digits and finds my sweet spot, my head drops back.

"Okay, will you please let them know I'll be arriving at ten?"

Nodding, knowing he can't see me, I cough, clearing my throat.

"Of course. I'll"—I inhale a deep breath as Franco suckles my clit into his mouth—"find... I mean... update your calendar. Their calendar."

"Are you sure you're okay, Rai?"

Teeth nibble my hardened nub, teasing the orgasm that's now tightening everything below my belly button.

"Yes, yes..." The last word is a hiss and I shut my eyes as Franco sinks a third finger, rubbing against my slick inner walls and sending me over. "Fine." With that, I drop the phone onto the cradle, hanging up on Carlos as my orgasm splinters through me. "Fuck!" I bite out as my body convulses, and my man licks up every sticky drop of my release.

SNEAK PEEK

Tainted Sins

MATTEO

There never was a time when I felt at ease with relationships. I didn't think anything of it when I was younger. It was easier to fuck around and ignore the nagging in my gut that I would need to find a wife at some point. There has to be heirs.

My phone buzzes in my pocket, and I pull it out to find Gio's name flashing on screen. Before I answer, I glance up to see Adri in the ocean. Her tanned skin glistening under the warm sunshine.

"What?"

"You need to come home." His voice is urgent, filled with concern. Being a twin means you can *feel* what the other person is experiencing. Not completely, but a niggling.

"What's happened?"

"We're heading to Chicago," he tells me. There are a few families out there. With Mason Gianetti, our cousin living in the city, I know we have connections, but I haven't seen the bastard in years.

"What's happened, Gio?"

"Mason needs our help," he tells me. "The plane should

be able to get you back by morning." The panic in his voice is rising with every passing moment. I wonder briefly if there is danger, or if Gio is making it out to be worse than it is. Either way, I can't refuse.

"Fine. I'll get Adri set up here and return alone." I don't need her in danger if there is a threat. And having her here in our home will make things easier. I don't have to worry if she's safe.

"See you soon." Gio hangs up and I'm left staring at the phone. Sometimes, he can be a pain in my ass. But I love him all the same.

Pushing to my feet, I sigh as I step out onto the white sand. She's not going to be happy about this, but work calls.

Franco's cousin, Mason Gianetti, has his own book. If you'd like another fix of mafia, one click BOUND.
Meet the Mafia Prince, Mason...

Sign up for my newsletter and receive a free novella from me.

Keep reading for an excerpt of Bound...

SNEAK PEEK - BOUND

PROLOGUE - MASON

It's been years since I first did it.

When the need to have someone fear me took hold and I became a man who didn't care who the fuck he hurt. But now it's different. I have a woman I love. Only, she wants more than I think I can give her.

This club is my castle, and sweet Savvie is my queen. My past never allowed me freedom, and to this day, I'm still bound to the life I grew up in. Still linked to the addiction that runs rife through my veins. The problem is, Savannah doesn't know about my dark past.

Seven Sins has become my salvation in so many ways, but as much as I try to hide the person I was, it fights back with a vengeance. I may not have wanted it, but I can no longer hide. I'm bound by a code. It has a hold over me and always will.

Stalking into my office, I shut the door and lock it. Savvie will walk in, and I can't have her seeing me like this. She's been an angel to put up with my shit. My lies have caught up to me, and I can't do anything to stop them seeping into her life.

I don't know what to do.

For the first time in my life, I'm at a loss.

When I first met her, I was enamored with the blonde beauty who was so different from the girls I grew up knowing. She gripped me more than any submissive I'd ever come across. Her desires filtered into my life, and I found myself aching when I wasn't near her. I was hungry for her each second of the day.

I knew I had to claim her.

Before her, I was a man with no emotions.

Cold.

Heartless.

Rabid.

I'd worked hard to prove to my father that I'm the son he always wanted, but I let him down when I watched him die in front of me. I was meant to step into his shoes, but I couldn't. I allowed my cousin the responsibility instead. It's wrong, I should never had done it, but that life was something I wanted to put behind me, the same way Carrick did with his. Only mine wasn't as easy.

With the news I received this morning, I know I can't hide who I am from Savvie anymore. And what scares me the most is, when she learns what I've been hiding, she'll finally walk away.

I know she's been waiting for a ring. And I want to give it to her, but I believe she deserves better than me. Four years, and I've hidden myself from her. Her past is dotted with the violence that stole everything from her. And I now know that I can't bring her into my own dark world.

Sighing, I open the drawer and pull out what I need.

There's never been so much as an inkling from her side that she knows. It has taken me years to perfect my double life. When Cristiano needed me, I was there. Not because I felt guilty for having him run an organization I should've been, but because I have the bloodlust.

I'm bound by my need.

As I bind my beautiful woman each night, I feel her agony and desire. It's a driving force behind me.

I love her.

I want her.

But I can never fully allow myself to give in to it. Knowing that I'll never be good enough for her has kept me at a distance.

I know I need to let Savannah go. But I'm a selfish bastard. Arrogant, filled with pride. But I know at some point the truth will spill free and there's nothing I can do to stop it. It's nothing new to me. The moment she stepped into the club, I realized the future for us was bleak. I couldn't help myself though. I ached to take her, and I did. Now, as my life comes to a head, there's so much she'll learn about me, about who I really am.

She'll leave.

And I know, when that day comes, I'll be lost.

I won't survive.

ARE YOU NEEDING MORE? ONE CLICK TO FIND OUT ALL THE SECRETS!

Click here for a full list of Dani René's incredible titles

About the Author

Dani is a *USA Today* Bestselling Author of seductive and deviant romance.

Her books range from the dark to emotional, but every hero is alpha, and each heroine is strong-willed, bringing the men down to their knees.

She now lives in the UK, after moving from Cape Town, exploring cemeteries and old buildings while plotting her next book.

When she's not writing, she can be found binge-watching the latest TV series, or working on graphic design. She has a healthy addiction to reading, tattoos, coffee, and ice cream.

www.danirene.com
info@danirene.com
Spotify